KINGSTON

A FOUR FATHERS STORY

DANI RENÉ

Kingston (Four Fathers #2)
Copyright © 2018 by Dani René
eBook ISBN - 978-0-639-93662-8
Print ISBN - 978-0-6399366-3-5
Cover Design: All By Design
Photo: DepositPhoto
Editor: Word Nerd Editing
Formatting: Raven Designs

The following story contains mature themes, strong language, and sexual situations. It is intended for adult readers.

I am arrogant. Insatiable. A single father.

I desire things that would make most people blush.
Normally, I find outlets that allow me to free the sexual beast living within and play to my heart's content.
And when my voluptuous, innocent assistant starts starving me after a little taste, I decide I'll let my inner animal feed—on her.
Trouble is, once I have her, I can't let her go, and that makes things complicated.

My name is Levi Kingston.

I am a dirty, ravenous, greedy man.
People may detest my kinks, but it doesn't stop them from wanting me.

DEDICATION

To my girls who love the filthy alphas I write.
This one's especially for you!

ONE

LEVI

I DON'T REMEMBER A TIME WHEN I DIDN'T GET WHAT I want.

I'm an asshole in every sense of the word.

I don't deny it, and I don't under any circumstances apologize for it. It's who I am, and if you don't like it, tough.

I live my life the way I do business.

Confident, shrewd, and calculated.

Even though I don't need to work, I do. It keeps my mind occupied. I'm one of the investors in Four Father's Freight, which allows me something other than my wayward teenage son to worry about. Also, when I'm in constant meetings, dealing with millions of dollars in contracts, I forget the day I said goodbye to my wife. She didn't leave me. Not by choice anyway. I spent six months by her side as cancer slowly riddled its way through her body and she gave up the fight.

That was eight years ago.

Now, I'm an asshole who fucks anything with a set of tits and a sweet, tight cunt. Yes, I admit it. My friends know who I am, what I do, and I make no apology for it. I've decided to enjoy my life, no connections, just pleasure. And having a pretty woman kneeling for me, ready to take my dick in her mouth is all I want and need.

The day I buried Abigail was the day I locked my heart away. The only thing that matters more to me in life besides the business is my son. Ethan is eighteen now, off to college soon, and even though we never see eye to eye, I love him.

He looks just like his mother. And perhaps that's why I've become closed off. When he looks at me with her hazel eyes, it's no longer with love and affection, it's disdain. I know he is angry, for his mother dying, for his father being a dick, and for life in general.

I want him to study something worthy of a career, but he's fought me tooth and nail. His interests are like this mother's—art, painting, sculpture. He's always been creative, even from a young age, but that's not going to put food on the table when he gets married and has a family to support.

Strolling into the office, I notice Eric's door is closed. His voice booms through the wood, which causes me to wonder whether he's talking to one of his son's or a client. I don't know how he deals with four boys; I can barely handle Ethan.

Shoving the door to my office open, I step inside to find Kristyn, my assistant, sitting at my desk, jotting notes on the small pad I keep at my computer. I call her mine because I was the one who found her, hired her, and showed her the ropes of how our business operates. Even though she handles the bookings and meeting schedules for all four of the partners, she's still mine.

Her long, glossy chestnut hair is pinned in a loose bun at the back of her head and small, black-rimmed glasses are perched on her button nose. She looks like a librarian with that innocent face and red apple cheeks, but when she bites down on her lower lip in concentration, my mind fills with images I shouldn't be having about my assistant.

Her three-month stint with Four Father's has been good. She's proven herself. When I interviewed her, she had a storm brewing in her pretty blue eyes, something hidden, and I decided then I'd make her my own personal project. I wanted to know what this almost nerdy girl was hiding beneath her prim exterior.

She may seem sweet and innocent, but she has sass that shocks the shit out of me at times. And for that, I respect her. Working with four alpha men can't be easy, but she's taken to it easily and gives as much as she gets.

I've been dying to bend her over my desk since she first walked into my office, not only because she's beautiful—she is that and so much more—but I want to learn about this little twenty-one-year-old.

"Good morning," I interrupt her train of thought, and her gaze snaps to mine in surprise. Big blue eyes, the color of the sky on a clear day, peer up at me.

"Mr. Kingston," she purrs my name. I know it's not done purposely, but there's a hint of need in her voice linked directly to my cock. "I was...I just finished your list for today."

She rises. Her blouse, a soft shade of blue matching her eyes, looks almost see-through, and I can't stop my gaze from dropping to the lace bra cupping her pert little tits.

She's everything a man could want and need. A pretty fuck toy for pleasure. I wonder how well she'd do being ordered around in the bedroom. Or bent over my desk, perhaps, while her tight, little cunt pulses around every inch of my cock.

"Would you like a coffee?" she questions while

rounding my desk. That's when I finally get a good look at her. Dressed in a black pencil skirt stopping just above her knees, she looks professional, yet utterly sinful. The material hugs her thighs and hips, taunting me from where she's standing.

Her shoes are higher than what's considered appropriate for work, but I can't deny how much I like the way they elongate her legs and show off her toned calves. Imagining her in just those heels and nothing else...my cock stirs behind the zipper of my slacks once more.

"Please," I finally respond, stalking by her toward my desk. A hint of lavender plumes around me, and I inhale the scent of her perfume, long and deep. She doesn't need to know she affects me. There's no rule stating I can't date or fuck her, but I've learned mixing business with pleasure is a no-no.

She doesn't say anything more before strolling from my office, her hips swaying left to right. There's a sensuality about her that brings out a primal need within me. I've been spending more hours at the office than I need just to see her each day.

Once I'm alone, I sit back and turn on the computer. The screen illuminates and reminders pop up, each with a ding, until I notice the last one. I'm meeting one of my biggest clients, Brent Masterson, tomorrow evening at Sizzle, one of the Michelin star restaurants downtown. Dinner and drinks with one of the country's most influential men.

As much as I'd rather spend the evening at home with a drink and cigar, this is an important client. His transport business will allow us to make use of his fleet for certain areas of the country.

Once he's signed the deal, there'll be more media surrounding us than a celebrity at the Oscar's ceremony. And there's nothing like media to skyrocket attention on the company.

My door flies open, and I glance up, finding Eric

looking overly confident with a smirk on his face.

"Hey, Pearson," I greet my best friend and partner. "What was that in there?" I nudge my chin toward the door, referring to his earlier heated phone conversation.

He sighs, flopping into the chair opposite my desk. "Brock. He's too old for his age."

"Tell me about it. Ethan's decided he's going to take a gap year without my knowledge. I overheard him on the phone last night." I can't help griping about my son. I've given him everything he's asked for, but each time I think I'm making some headway, I lose my footing. It's been like that since he turned thirteen.

"Join me tonight? I'm meeting Sanders and his associate for a business powwow," he informs me with a salacious grin on his face. Settling himself into the seat opposite my desk, he continues. "I told him you might be there. The last time we had drinks together, he signed that five-mil deal."

He's right. Sanders was an easy target to seal, and the

money went straight into the company, putting us at the top of the list in the freight and shipping industry. After that deal, we had five new clients wanting to sign million-dollar contracts for our services.

I'm about to respond when Kristyn appears at the door. I crook my finger to call her in, not missing the blush on her cheeks. Her full lips glisten as she makes her way toward the desk.

Her eyes fall to Eric, and the color on her cheeks deepens. Jealousy rears its head, and for the first time in a long while, I wonder if this innocent little girl is really getting to me.

"Good morning, Mr. Pearson. Would you like—"

"No, thank you," Eric interrupts her, waving his hand, but his cold blue eyes trail hungrily over her curves. She nods, offering him a small smile as she sets my mug down. Eric is too old for her. At least...that's what I tell myself. We're the same age, but for some reason, she's not off limits to me.

"Thank you. That's all," I dismiss her. She only offers me a smile before she heads out, shutting the door behind her. I turn my attention back to Eric. "So, you need me to babysit you on this meeting tonight?" I taunt, earning a deep chuckle.

"Fuck you, Kingston," he retorts. "Besides, it won't be me you're watching." I tilt my head to the side in question. "He wants to meet at Poison."

The corner of my mouth kicks into a smirk as I steeple my fingers under my chin and watch Eric's face. The infamous strip club is known for the most elite business meetings that take place while receiving a lap dance or private show. They're strict. No touching. If you even lift a finger or a girl complains, you're out the door and banned for life.

"That's the place you've been wanting to go to since it opened three months ago. Isn't it?"

He pins me with a knowing stare. A swift nod, then he narrows his eyes. "You're the one who suggested it a few weeks ago. And I heard those tight teen pussies are always up for an extra tip or two." He shrugs noncommittally, but the predatory grin on his face tells me more.

"Make sure your wallet is stacked. I'm sure they'd love to feel how thick and bulging it is," I throw back, chuckling at his grin.

"I'll ensure the bulge they're feeling is the right one." His hand falls to his crotch as he grips it. He's the epitome of a manwhore. Eric Pearson is definitely not the man you take home to mommy and daddy.

Most of the clubs we frequent are filled with a bevy of beautiful, young women who would do anything to please. Just turned eighteen and so pliable. And Eric has a penchant for pretty young things. The problem is he's always picking out the blonde plastic dolls. I'm more of a brunette man...like the woman just outside my office door.

"I take it that's a yes?" He quirks a dark eyebrow in question, and I know I have no choice. Not that I'd want one.

“Always.”

“It’s settled then,” he says, rising as he buttons his suit jacket. “See you later.”

He leaves me in the office to mull over what tonight will bring.

TWO

KRISTYN

PULLING UP MY BLACK THIGH-HIGHS, I CLIP THEM to the garter that hugs my waist. A soft, sensual silk negligee with lace trim covers my breasts, the hemline hitting just below my ass. It's my signature look. The men in the club generally go wild. The more skin on offer, the more I taunt and tease, the more money I make.

It's been almost two months and the tips have been just enough to get by. My life isn't easy. In fact, it's been a bitch. But I promised myself I could do it on my own. I'm not like my mother, who ran off with a man every week, only to return to my father and beg his forgiveness when her cash cow didn't pay out.

That's the last thing I need: a man to save me.

Over the years, I've learned if you can't do something

on your own, you shouldn't bring another into the equation. That's why I'm single. I focus on my job and make sure my dad is looked after. For as long as I can remember, it's just been me and him.

After the fourth time my mother fucked him over, he told her to turn around, walk out the door, and never come back. I was proud of him in that moment, reminding myself that leaning on someone to get you through something is not how to live.

And love.

That's a pointless institution.

I don't believe in it. If someone ever uttered that word to me, he'd be out the door faster than he could blink. No. I spend three nights a week dancing, making enough to pay the bills. The extra money comes in handy when my father's medical expenses skyrocket with each treatment.

Casting a quick glance in the mirror, I add my final touch: a deep ruby lipstick that makes my lips look even more plump than they already are. Men love this shit.

Sex sells.

There's a reason porn is such a wide industry. Men are visual creatures, and the more I can entice them, the more bills I see in my purse at the end of the day.

One last glance at my reflection and I nod to the girl looking back at me. It's these nights I don't recognize her. Sadness holds me hostage for a moment before I shake it off and rise on my *fuck-me* heels.

The night is warm and filled with promise. I hear them enter, and make my way down the ornate staircase. Glancing up, I take note of the three men standing in the host area talking to Henriette about a private room for a business meeting. When I near them, three sets of eyes shoot up, taking me in as I strut by.

My breathing hitches as a set of familiar dark eyes pierce me. The beat of my heart matches that of the song playing in the background—wild and fast. Praying he doesn't recognize me, I turn away and walk into the main area of the club. It's not one of those large chain clubs. This is an intimate place where men come to unwind.

No touching is allowed. And that's the only reason I haven't walked out. I've overheard horror stories that would turn the strongest woman into a trembling mess. However, Henriette is like a vulture. With the team of bodyguards who watch over us, I feel safe here.

The gazes of the men in the foyer burn into me as I pass. Heat trickles over my long legs and ass barely covered by the black negligee. When I reach the bar, Judas, our barman, glances my way, offering a slight nod.

"The regular?" he asks, talking about my drink. I nod. "It's going to be busy tonight," he says in a faraway tone that hints at his hatred for this place. It's no secret he and his girlfriend are here out of necessity, not enjoyment.

"It will be," I respond, but I don't give a shit. I'm here for one reason. It's been almost six weeks and this place has offered me a way out of debt. I don't have much else to offer him in response, so I pick up my drink and head over to the table where the girls sit.

Three beautiful, young women who have their whole lives ahead of them. Sadly, we all have a reason to be here. Whether it's to pay off student loans or get away from an abusive boyfriend, we all find our way into Poison.

"Kismet," one of the girls, I think her name is Onyx, smiles up at me, and I lift my glass in greeting. "You look gorgeous," she says with a glistening gaze. It's been a long while since I've been with a woman. I recall a few nights while I attended community college filled with parties and alcohol. That was before my dad got sick.

"Thank you." I don't tell her she looks good, because there's no point. I'm not here to make friends. I keep them all at an arm's length. Perhaps that's why I'm so lonely. Rather than having a big group of fake friends, I'd rather spend time at home with a good book.

Most nights when I'm not working, that's where I am. Cuddled up in a big, floppy tee with the latest romance novel. Reading about sex and having it are very different things. Most people don't know I'm still a virgin.

I down the gin and tonic with a wince before making my way to the foyer where I find Henriette typing away on the computer. Her gray hair is knotted in a severe bun at the back of her head and her kind, chocolate eyes hold affection for all her girls. Her sturdy build always reminds me of my gran who used to give the best hugs. Henriette is about fifty, but doesn't allow age to play a factor in the way she enjoys her time with us girls.

"Darling," she smiles up at me. "You have a private dance request. They only requested you," she tells me with a frown. Most men who have business meetings ask for more girls to entertain them, but I guess I'll be on my own tonight.

"I just need to use the restroom, then I'll head in to VIP," I inform her. A small smile is my response as I head by her and down the hall toward the bathroom. They are so beautifully decked out, they look like they were transported from a five-star hotel. Before I reach the entrance, a hand shoots out, gripping my arm.

"Kristyn?" My heart stops. When I turn to look into familiar mocha eyes, my throat closes with anxiety.

Shit. He did recognize me.

I'm wearing a wig that covers my normally chestnut waves in a sleek raven-colored curtain, but those eyes penetrate me. They see past the façade, finding the hidden girl normally in his office.

Shaking my head, I glare at him. "Wrong girl," I utter in a low voice, hearing the trepidation in my tone. I'm hoping he'll release me—pray he'll realize his mistake.

But I know he won't.

He can't.

Because I am her.

I am the girl he orders around every day. The same girl who schedules his meetings and knows exactly how he likes his coffee. My tension skyrockets when he leans in farther without letting go. He inhales me, as if he can sniff out my lie.

"It is you," he utters in shock. His gaze drinks me in like a fine wine, savoring every drop. When those dark orbs land on the spot inside my arm, I'm done for. My truth is clear. Levi Kingston saw my tattoo when I walked into the office one day because I'd forgotten my phone at work. It was a Saturday, and I didn't think anyone would be there, but as soon as he exited his office, I was hooked.

I was dressed in my workout clothes—a tiny sports bra and tights—since I'd been out jogging. It was then he saw the tattoo on my arm normally covered in my office attire.

The small ink of a bird in flight has been on my flesh for four years. I got it when I turned seventeen. It was rebellious—the only *bad* thing I'd ever done. I'd never touched drugs, or even had a drop of alcohol. And boyfriends? Well, they were non-existent.

His gaze roams over me, hinting at the sexual tension between us I already knew was evident. Since the first day I walked into his office, I was too aware of him—of how he made me feel.

And every day since, I've pushed it to the back of my mind. He's too good for me. A successful man like him must have women draping themselves over him at every opportunity.

How could he look at an innocent girl half his age in *that* way?

He doesn't say another word. Instead, he shoves me into the restroom, shutting and locking the door behind him. Levi has always been a force to be reckoned with, and I could never fight him off. Not that I would. I want him to touch me—to manhandle me. I want to be at his beck and call. I don't know why. I can't explain it, but the man exudes sex, hunger, and raw, animalistic desire.

Like a hurricane taking down a city, he destroys me every moment I'm close to him. Each time I'm near him is another second I lose myself. We're from two different worlds, and they can never clash. My life is too complicated. This innate desire I feel for Levi needs to stay where it is in the back of my mind.

"You should leave," I tell him. My voice is assertive, but the way I shiver in fear, wariness, and desire doesn't go unnoticed. I've been sassy with him before, offering my opinion when I think something won't work. But this right here...this is different.

"Kristyn, why are you here?" His question is something I can't answer. There's no way I can afford him with the truth.

"This is my time out of the office. I don't answer to you here," I inform him, lifting my chin, attempting to find the confidence I don't feel.

"Like fuck you don't," he growls. His voice is a rumble of torturous yearning that sounds pained. *Why would it matter to him what I do?*

"Levi...Mr. Kingston, this is my life. I don't need you to save me. I don't need a knight in shining armor to care what I do when I'm not on the clock." I place my hands on his chest, wanting to push him away, but I don't.

Heated tingles shoot through my body at the contact. His shirt is warm beneath the material. His taut muscles feel glorious under my fingertips.

"Kristyn, don't fucking test me right now," he spits out, the words full of frustration. He's on me in seconds, ensuring I can't escape. His hands plant on either side of my head against the wall, pinning my back flush against the cool tiles, forcing a gasp to fall from my lips.

"I wasn't testing you." My response is nothing more than a whimpering moan. Chastising myself, I push against his body, hoping he'll let up, but he doesn't. Instead, he leans in, his mouth inches from mine.

My core pulses, a heavy ache tightening low in my gut. I'm turned on by his possessiveness.

I want this. I want him.

"I gave you a job. Wasn't it good enough? You come here to shake your ass in front of assholes who pay you too?" His voice holds more anguish than anger.

"Yet, here you are, asshole." My retort has his gaze

lighting up like an inferno. It burns into me. Fire blazing through a forest, taking down everything in its path.

His hands grip my shoulders and he spins me around before shoving me back against the wall. My face presses hard against the surface.

"What are you doing?" My words are muffled by the porcelain. Soft hues of cream and pink are too close to my face.

"I'm showing you what an *asshole* I can be," he growls, lifting the negligee to bunch around my hips. Without warning, he swats my ass painfully, the sting eliciting a whimper from me. He rains down another, and another, until my knees buckle.

I haven't been spanked since I was a kid. But this is very different. This...this just made me wet, my arousal soaking the flimsy material of my panties. And I wonder just what else Mr. Kingston can and would want to do to me. Those thoughts have my belly fluttering with hummingbird wings. I've wanted him since the first day I walked into his office. But it can never work. There's just no way... or is there?

THREE

LEVI

"THAT'S WHAT AN ASSHOLE CAN DO," I TELL HER, releasing her from my grip.

She turns to glare at me, and I can't stop my cock from throbbing. The need to shove her to her knees and feed her my dick runs rampant through my veins. She's incredible. Exquisite in the tiny lingerie hugging every fucking curve of her beautiful body.

"Do you realize Eric is here too? If he saw you tonight..." I don't have to finish the sentence. She knows this could ensure she gets fired from Four Father's. Her job is on the line because she wants men to look at her.

"I...I didn't think about it."

"No, you didn't fucking think." My words are harsh, and I immediately want to take them back at her wince.

A knock on the door interrupts us. "Are you okay in there, Kismet?" It's the old lady from the reception area. I snap my gaze to Kristyn and pin her with a glare, telling her to get rid of the woman.

"I'll be out in a minute," she calls to her boss.

"All right, hurry. The clients would like to get started."

Once we're alone, I grip her arm and tug her against me. I don't know why, but the need to hold her makes me do stupid shit. "You'll go out there, tell her you're not feeling well, and go home."

"I can't—"

"That's a fucking order from your boss. Do it," I command in a no-nonsense tone. She peeks up at me with those big blue eyes, and I almost lose it. I reign in the desire to fuck her right here on the spot, holding onto it until I get her alone—until I have hours to show her how much of an asshole I can really be.

"Fine. But you're paying me the money I would've earned tonight." She crosses her arms in front of her chest, which doesn't help the fact that I want my dick between those luscious tits while her tongue laps at the arousal on the crown.

"I'll pay you that and more. Just get your ass out of here," I hiss, my frustration blooming into a darkened hurricane that wants to tear this little girl apart. She peeks up at me with a fragility that tugs at my chest. Her curvaceous frame in next to nothing is what wet dreams are made of—especially mine.

She stalks by me, her hips swaying hypnotically. I know she's doing it on purpose, trying to bait me to devour her, and I will certainly do that. Now that I've had a taste, I want more. The click of the door alerts me that I'm alone. Sighing, I glance in the mirror.

Breathing through the range of emotions, I wait until my hard-on is gone before I head out to the main area of the club. I find Sanders and his business associate at the bar, along with Pearson, their drinks already ordered.

"You ready? Thought you got lost." Eric glares at me,

curiosity in his blue eyes.

Shrugging, I reach for my Scotch, down it in one gulp, and order another. "I'm fine," I murmur before glancing at him. "Let's get this show on the road."

"That, my dear boy, sounds like a splendid idea," Sanders chuckles, and we follow him into the private room he requested.

As soon as we're settled on the plush velvet sofas, the hostess strolls in. "Gentlemen, I'm sorry to say Kismet isn't feeling well this evening, but I have two lovely ladies to keep you entertained."

My heart kicks in my chest at the mention of her stage name. Eric's gaze burns into the side of my face. Leaning in, he whispers, "Does *Kismet* being ill have something to do with you, Kingston?" The amusement in his tone has me overly aware that he must've seen me with her earlier.

Thankfully, she was wearing a wig. He wouldn't have recognized her because of that one minor detail.

"What do you mean?" I glare at Pearson. The asshole

is too intuitive for his own good. Also, he's a hound. He'd fuck Kristyn if he knew she was single, or if he knew I wanted her. The man is great at business, but he'll fuck any young pussy that comes his way.

"I know you too well, Levi. You can have any beauty on your dick in seconds," he chuckles. He's right, I can. Lifting his tumbler, he tips it my way, then swallows down the amber liquid.

"It's not like you're an angel, Pearson. Your dick is overused. You need to tone it down some," I bite back in jest. We both guffaw at the sentiments that fit the other perfectly. I've never had close friends. None that I'd feel comfortable talking to like this, anyway. The guys I went to college with were all prep school boys. Too fucking posh for their own good. They wouldn't know what to do with a pussy if one was handed to them on a silver platter.

A moment later, two beautiful dancers with next to nothing covering their tits and cunt stroll in. With bodies that would make a priest break his vows, and lips that would make a sane man lose his mind, they take the small stage and begin a routine to *Cookie* by R. Kelly.

The sexual song and their swaying hips have my cock responding, but my mind is still with Kristyn and the way her ass reddened with my handprint.

"Who's on your mind, Kingston?" Eric thuds me on the shoulder, his piercing eyes boring into me with curiosity.

"Nobody." My response is clipped, almost angry. I know I need to shut the fuck up before he figures it out, but with him goading me like he normally does, I don't know if I can. I'm still worked up from earlier with that sweet little vixen.

"Like fuck will I believe that. Who is she?"

I keep my gaze trained on the two beauties swirling and twirling before us. One of them steps off the stage, heading right for Eric. She places her pert ass on his lap, grinding on the bulge prominent in his slacks.

"Hi, handsome," she utters from those plump—surely Botox—lips.

He turns to her, not the least bit interested. She's trying her utmost to get something out of him. Her hands trail up his thighs, landing on his crotch. "You'll have to do so much more than palm my dick to get a decent tip," he tells her with confidence. Her big green eyes widen in shock. "I don't do well with teases."

"We're not allowed—"

He leans in, getting as close to her has he can without touching her. "I didn't say I wanted to touch you, sweetheart. Those plastic tits do nothing for me," he informs her with a dark, condescending tone that causes her to huff.

"Stop pissing off the girls, Pearson." Sanders' gruff tone filters over to us from the other side of the room. The space is small. So much so, the girls could easily reach him while sitting on our laps.

"Let's talk business," I chirp, hoping to get this done

and dusted. As soon as I walk out of this place, my next stop is Kristyn's house. I don't give a shit how late it is, she'll be explaining what the fuck she's doing taking her clothes off for men like Sanders.

The second dancer rises from Holloway, the business associate seated beside our client. Sanders drops a folder on the stage situated between us, and I lean over to pick it up. Opening it, I find the figures we asked them for. They're looking to sign a contract with us for the next five years that brings in almost ten-billion.

Handing the paperwork to Eric, I watch as he glances over the pages. He lifts his gaze, meeting mine with a satisfied smirk. "Think you can have a few more of these meetings as we seal the deal?" he questions.

The blonde dancer, who is all natural from her tits to her lips, settles herself on my lap. I cast a quick glance at her, but my dick doesn't twitch. Not even when she grinds her perfect ass on my lap. She's no Kristyn.

"I think I can deal with it," I tell my partner, then look

over at Sanders. "And this contract, it will be exclusive to us. We sign now, we get the deal. You're not shopping around, or looking for a *shared* operation?" I ask him. He's shrewd—an overzealous businessman who will chuck his money at anyone who does his dirty work.

"You're the only company I've come to with it."

There's not a flicker of dishonesty. I nod. "Fine." I lift my glass. "It's a deal." Barbie is still sitting on my lap when I down my drink.

"Lovely. Four Father's will be my go to for all future dealings if this goes well." Our new client grins like a fucking Cheshire cat. He's old, probably in his early seventies, with a rounding belly and balding head. He reminds me of a pervy grandpa you would normally warn your daughters not to take candy from. Those small, beady eyes, dark as night, are almost sinister, but he's worth millions, billions even, so as long as he is on board, we'll be just fine.

"There's no reason it won't, Sanders," Eric tells him.

Sighing, I glance at Eric. “Is that all you needed me here for?”

“Why? Got a tight little hole wet and ready for you at home?” Eric questions, his eyebrow arching. He lifts his refilled Scotch, taking it like a shot as he necks it in one gulp.

“Not at home, but I will be inside her tonight,” I finally admit, knowing he wouldn’t give up if I didn’t give him something. He loves hearing about what I do to the pretty young things with rope and a paddle. Reddening porcelain ass cheeks, ensuring they’re whimpering, mewling for me to fuck them, then, finally, driving deep inside their tight bodies while I torture their nipples and clits with metal clamps.

Something tells me I should invite my friend to the BDSM club I’ve frequented over the past few months. Perhaps he can work his way through the beauties dying for an asshole to spank and fuck them.

He offers me a knowing grin and slaps me on the

shoulder while the pretty dancer stands up, knowing she's not doing it for me. "I knew there had to be something stealing your attention."

"Not so much my attention, but she's definitely intrigued me," I tell him.

"Well, you better get going. And if you get your dick wet, and it's good, ask if she has a sister," he murmurs conspiratorially.

"You're an asshole, Pearson," I retort.

"Takes one to know one, Kingston," he bites back as I rise from my seat.

Buttoning up my suit jacket, I offer a nod toward our client. "I'll see you in the office tomorrow to finalize the contracts."

"Good. I look forward to it." Sanders shakes my hand. I don't bother looking at his associate, who looks like a teenager trying to play in the adult's world. Striding from the room, I step into the main area of the club, which is now filled with suits. Their eyes are trained on the stages where women grind against poles and kneel, taunting the men for more money.

Shaking my head, I exit the club. The night is chilly. Pulling my phone from my pocket, I tap out a message to Kristyn. Something tells me she's still awake. I don't tell her I'm coming over. Instead, I wish her a good night.

Slipping into the driver's seat of my BMW X5, I start the engine and pull out onto the road. I know where she lives, her address was on her resume and I found myself memorizing it. At the time, I didn't think I'd need it the way I do right now. What I don't know is if she's alone or has a boyfriend. However, the whimpers I elicited from her plump lips earlier tell me she does not.

Her heat was intoxicating. There's always been sexual tension between us, but what happened in the restroom confirms she wants me. Even if she did have a boyfriend, I'd fuck her so hard, until my dick was the only one she craved.

I don't give a shit if there's anyone else in her life.

Tonight, she's mine.

FOUR

KRISTYN

THE HOUSE I SHARE WITH MY DAD ISN'T HUGE, BUT it's comfortable. I grew up in this home, and when he got sick, leaving wasn't an option. He's been here for me all my life, supporting me, giving me a chance at a career of my dreams, so I stayed to be his support.

I learned early on, though, all those hopes you hold onto and work toward don't always happen. And slowly, I've come to terms with that. My heart sinks as I think about things I've had to let go of, dropping my bag on the living room table, I head into the kitchen to grab a bottle of sparkling water from the fridge.

"Krissy, what are you doing home so early?" Dad's voice comes from behind me. My gaze lands on him, and I breathe a sigh of relief when I notice he looks better than he has in a long while.

"I wasn't feeling well," I tell him, noticing the immediate concern on his face. "I'm okay now, Dad. I promise." I lean in and place a soft peck on his cheek. My father isn't overly affectionate, but I know he loves me in his own way.

"Good. I'm heading to bed," he tells me. "Don't stay up too late." Every night since I was thirteen and needed to be up for school the next morning, he's told me the same thing. And each time, I respond the same way.

"I won't, Dad. Love you." He waves away my words and I smile. He's fragile. As he ages, my heart aches knowing our time is running out. The doctors said it could be six months, or might be a year, but each day, he will wither. Watching someone you love—someone who was so strong for so long—lose a fight with their health is painful.

The click of his bedroom door tells me I'm alone with my thoughts of what happened at the club. Seeing Levi there was a shock to my system. I reveled in his concern, but having him recognize me was scarier. I thought for sure he was going to fire me. When he told me to come home, I figured it would be the end of my career at Four Fathers' Freight, but he only did it to get me away from Eric Pearson.

Mr. Pearson is somewhat of an asshole. Rude. Arrogant. And utterly disgusting at times. Like when he leers at my chest, or I feel him staring at my ass, burning a hole through the material of my skirt. If he knew I was a dancer, I'm certain he'd have done much worse than spank me.

Eric probably would have fucked me right there in the toilet stall and wouldn't have been satisfied until I screamed his name. I've overheard him and Levi talking in the office about their conquests. And as much as I am horrified by some of the things I've overheard, I've also been turned on more than ever by Levi Kingston.

The two men are predators.

Rich, powerful, and so handsome, it's almost illegal.

They both dress impeccably, but it's always Levi who catches my eye. He causes my heart to race erratically. And most times, my panties are wet when he pins me with those dark, hungry eyes.

Curling up on the sofa, I pick up my latest romance novel and open it to the next chapter. The story has me hooked, and I can't wait to find out what happens next. My eyes are roaming the pages eagerly when a knock on the door startles me.

Frowning, I glance at the wall clock, noticing it's well past eleven. Quickly, I rise and head toward the door as another few raps sound. Twisting the handle, I tug open the door an inch to peer out the crack.

My lips part on a shocked gasp when I'm met with familiar dark eyes. They eat me up, from my head down to my toes, then back up.

"What are you doing here?" I ask quietly. My eyes are glued to Levi and his feral expression.

"I'm here to talk." Even though he says those words, I don't believe them. The glint in his gaze is mischievous. Wolfish. As if he can get me to do anything he wants, and he possibly can with just a snap of his fingers.

"But—"

"Open the damn door, Kristyn, or should I call you *Kismet*?" he quips, the corner of his mouth lifting into a knowing smirk.

Sighing, I close the door, unlatch the metal chain, and pull it open for him to step inside. "You shouldn't be here," I whisper, hoping my father has already fallen asleep. I don't need to be answering to two men tonight.

"Why are you whispering?" Levi glances around, taking in my comfortable living room, which I'm sure is far smaller than his. The men who own Four Fathers are all wealthy and live in the most beautiful homes in Florida.

Mansions I've only ever seen on TV or in magazines with gardens that could fit my whole house and more.

"My father is asleep," I tell him. My attempt at getting away from him is hindered when his hand shoots out, grasping my wrist. "Levi," I utter his name, lifting my blue eyes to meet his dark ones. There's a storm brewing in them, and I wonder if he's going to wreck me as much as I'm certain he can.

"I need to talk to you. Eric was asking questions about you," he tells me in a hushed whisper. "Well...the dancer. I managed to sway him off the interrogation, but I know he won't let it go." He releases me.

The urgency in his tone is clear. I could have gotten into trouble. I could've lost my job, and that would've been detrimental. I need the job. I need them both. It's the only way I can afford to live. That's none of Levi's business, though. My private life is just that: mine.

"I've been thinking about it, and I have a proposition for you," he utters, and I snap my gaze to his in shock. "You said you needed the money." I nod. "And I guess you're not going to tell me why?" I shake my head *no*. I would respond, but I can't find the words. My tongue feels thick, heavy, and the lump in my throat doesn't allow me to swallow. Anxiety weighs on my chest along with fear.

He watches me for a moment before stepping closer. The heat of his body envelops me, holding me hostage under his intense gaze. I can't stop my eyes from inching up his chest to his neck and the slightest dusting of stubble on his face.

My palms tingle to touch it. I wonder what it would feel like if his face was between my thighs. My cheeks heat in embarrassment as the images flit through my mind. He's my boss. Off limits. But it doesn't stop my thighs from squeezing together.

"Spend the month with me. As a..." he tips his head to the side, as if thinking about the right word to use, "companion. I need someone to accompany me to functions, as well as someone to come home to after a long, hard day," he utters in a husky tone which sends a shiver down my spine. The closeness of his body causes my body to react once more. His hands find purchase on my hips, tugging me closer, and my palms land on his chest.

"No." The word is a gasp falling in the space between us. "There's no way I can do that." Once again, I feel the heat of him under my touch. His body is solid, and I can't help reveling in the warmth. My attempt to push him away is fruitless. He doesn't budge. Something tells me it won't be so easy to rid myself of him.

"You can, and you will. You'll quit your job at the club, there'll be no more dancing for men. I'll transfer twenty-five-thousand dollars into your bank account in the morning," he says, no hint of jest in his tone. He's serious. Deathly so.

"I'm not a whore," I bite out angrily. Shaking my head, I meet his stare with a confident one of my own. "You cannot just walk into my house and offer me money to fuck you."

My words cause him to lean in close. "Listen to me, and listen very fucking carefully," he hisses, his mouth on the shell of my ear. "I'll do anything I want to you, *Kismet*." There's no anger in his tone as he bites out my stage name, but jealousy drips from the word like a poison.

"And what makes you think you can just order me around like I'm your slave?"

"This." He reaches between my thighs and cups my pussy. When his fingers press against my clit, I whimper. "That little mewl from your plump lips is all the evidence I need. You enjoy me ordering you around, and I do recall you being wet as fuck when I spanked your sweet ass in that restroom, so don't stand there telling me I don't affect you."

He's right. I can't deny it. I want this man. I ache for him to touch me, to make me moan his name as I unravel on his fingers and tongue and cock.

His teasing touch circles my clit. My body is ready, needy, and slick for him to dip into me. But he doesn't. He continues to torture me through my panties. There's no denying he's an expert at this. I'm fighting a losing battle.

"Now, tomorrow, you'll call your boss at that shit-show of a club and tell her you got another job." His voice is a demanding whisper. "Then, you'll get dressed and come to work. You'll bring me my coffee, schedule my meetings, and when you're done at the office..." he leans in farther, suckling my earlobe into his hot mouth, allowing his teeth to graze the flesh, "you'll come to my house where I will fuck you as punishment for turning me on so much."

He trails his mouth to my neck, biting down harshly, and I find myself wanting him to leave a mark there. I want him to hurt me.

"I'm not a nice man, little Kismet," he taunts with words and fingers. "I'm going to abuse your pretty little body until you can't move. Until the only thing you'll need, crave, and hunger for is my cock in your tight holes."

"You're right," I tell him, and he moves back, his eyes burning with desire. "You are an asshole," I bite out, tugging myself free of his hold. Stalking into the kitchen, I open the fridge and grab another bottle of chilled water. My body trembles with need for him. As filthy as his promises are, I find myself wanting them.

He follows me; I feel him before I hear him. He doesn't touch me, but it feels as if his hands are all over me. Goosebumps erupt over every inch of my skin at his nearness. Nothing has ever prepared me for the overbearing Levi Kingston. In the office, we're nothing more than boss and employee, but here, in the privacy of my home, he's a man I want inside me. I want his mouth on me, his lips suckling my flesh, marking me.

"Do you mean to tell me, if I fucked my fingers into you right now, you wouldn't drip all over my hand with those sweet juices currently coating your panties?" He tips his head to the side and scrutinizes me, and it feels as if I'm a mystery to him. The soft curve of his lips forms a smirk so sinful, I feel as if the devil is standing before me. Perhaps he is. Leading me into temptation.

"You need to leave," I tell him, setting the bottle on the counter. That was my mistake. He moves swiftly, his body pressing me against the edge of the counter, the thickness of his erection firm against my ass, nestling between the cheeks, perfectly taunting.

"Do you want me to leave, Kismet?" he asks, cooing the name along the sensitive skin behind my ear. One hand fists my long chestnut waves and tugs my head to the side, exposing my neck to his rabid mouth.

The wetness of his tongue trails along the flesh, tasting me from my collarbone to my ear, where he once again suckles, then bites down harder than earlier. His free hand tracks its way up to my nipple, tweaking it through the material of my tee. When he yanks it harshly, another whimper laced with desire echoes around us, breaking the silence.

"I thought so," he grits out through clenched teeth.

His jaw ticks wildly and I wonder if he's angry or turned on or is it a bit of both. Releasing me, he leaves me cold, shaky, and beyond turned on. I'm fucked. I'm in so deep right now, my mind is fogged with lust for the man I work for—the man who's standing in my kitchen with the biggest bulge I've ever felt—and I don't want him to leave.

I shake my head, attempting to clear the thoughts of what he can do to me—of what I *want* him to do to me. "You really do need to leave," I utter noncommittally, glancing down the hallway toward my father's bedroom door.

"I'll go. But I want you to remember one thing, baby girl. If you don't do as I say, I'll only force the issue. I want you. I will get you. And once you're mine, I'll make you come on my fingers anywhere I please."

He turns on his heel and stalks from the kitchen, leaving me whirling from the demanding force of Levi Kingston. The click of the front door sounds like a foghorn in the darkness and silence. I don't for one second doubt this man will not give up until I submit to his demands. The memory of him offering me twenty-five-thousand dollars filters into my thoughts. It's a lot of money. But what do I really have to lose? I want to refuse, but when I think of my father, my decision is easy.

FIVE

LEVI

WHAT THE FUCK AM I DOING?

That's the question that plagued me while I was standing in her kitchen, needing to be closer to her, to touch and taste her. And goddamn, if her father hadn't been in the same house, I would've made her come all over the kitchen table.

Reigning in my restraint was near impossible. My cock throbs painfully. My balls are heavy with my seed. Wanting to empty myself in her tight little holes is at the forefront of my mind as I drive home.

The late-night air is humid, stifling. Thankfully, the roads are quiet, because I'm not focused. I can't think straight. All I see is Kristyn. Pulling into the garage, I exit the car, still hard from my encounter with the brunette beauty. Her blue eyes shimmered with shock and innocence at my proposition, only serving to confirm I want her.

Entering the house, I find it quiet, empty. Ethan is probably asleep. He leaves tomorrow on a month-long tour of colleges. The gap year he's planning is still up for discussion. Once he's done figuring out which school he wants to attend, we'll relook his decision not to study once he's graduated.

Since he decided to move out of the house and study away from home, I find myself at odds. I wish he'd stay, but I can't force him. I recall my own parents who shoved me into the life they wanted for me, instead of asking me what I wanted, and vowed I'd never do that to him.

Since Abi's death, I became relaxed with him, so much so, one night I got home late from work and found him and his girlfriend at the time fucking on my sofa. His seventeen-year-old ass got grounded. I didn't want to see him doing that shit.

Although, I had to give it to him. He has great taste in women. The girl he was plowing was cute. Her pert little tits were delicious, and her cunt was shaven. I got an eyeful before she ran off to his bedroom to hide away.

That brings my thoughts back to Kristyn. Her body is petite in every way. She'd be perfect to fuck like a doll. Throwing her on my bed, watching her bounce on the soft mattress while her pert tits jiggled...

I need to calm the fuck down.

I'm not one for jerking off in the shower—or anywhere else, for that matter. If I need a fuck, I find it, but tonight, all I want to do is fist my dick with thoughts of her riding me.

Stalking down the hall toward my wing of the house, I shove open my bedroom door and step inside. The black and white furnishing fits perfectly with the modern design of the house. The clean lines and sleek silver with glass was elegantly done. I couldn't live in the house where Abi died, so when I bought this place, I ensured there wasn't an ounce of her left behind.

Memories are all I have, and they're enough to haunt me at every turn.

Unbuttoning my shirt, I shrug it off and toss it on the armchair near the window. The leather belt is next, along with my black slacks. Once I'm only in a pair of tight boxers, I settle back on the bed and close my eyes. My palm finds itself on my hard-on, gripping it through the material as I recall images of Kismet.

My sweet, delicious little girl.

She's so fucking innocent, I want to violate her in every way possible. The image of her on her knees swallowing my dick has me shoving my briefs down and fisting my dick.

Arousal from the tip of my cock trails its way down my shaft as I jerk off. My movements are fast and erratic, as if I can't get enough. Imagining her tight hole, slick and needy for me...my body shudders as my balls draw up, ready to empty themselves.

Spurts of hot seed shoot onto my bare stomach, drenching me while thoughts of her drift through my mind on a loop. There's something about this girl that's found its way into my head, taunting me at every turn.

I'm not sure what I'm going to do tomorrow when she walks into my home, but one thing is for damn sure: she'll be bent over taking my dick before the night is over. Grabbing tissues, I wipe up the mess I made and roll over onto my side. The red numbers on the clock beside my bed glare at me, telling me it's after midnight.

I shut my eyes, calling on sleep to allow me a reprieve from my pain. Guilt stirs over what I just did, and the need to do it again.

"Dad." Ethan's voice drags me from my slumber of blue eyes and chestnut waves. When I finally crack my eyes, I find my eighteen-year-old son staring at me from the bedroom door. "It's almost time for me to leave," he tells me, then turns to leave.

A quick glance at the clock informs me it's just after seven. I groan as I push off the bed, finding morning wood trying to escape my boxers. It's way too early for anything other than a strong cup of coffee, but I need to be supportive and show him I'll be here for him no matter what he decides.

I pull on gray sweats and a T-shirt, and head out to the living room where Ethan is finishing off his coffee. His dark hair is messy, standing in all directions, and his eyes, a deep brown matching his mother's, glance up when I enter.

"Are you looking forward to it?" I ask, heading into the kitchen. The open plan space allows him to respond while I busy myself with getting myself some java.

"I am," he tells me, joining me at the breakfast counter. Our kitchen is kitted out with the latest appliances, but I only use the coffeemaker and fridge. I'm not much of a cook, neither is my son, so we normally order in dinner.

"I'll miss you." I don't know where the words come from, but I utter them anyway. He glances at me in shock. I've never shown affection, never hugged him, or told him I love him, and I realize what an asshole that makes me. But saying those words only hurt more than they helped.

"Yeah. I'll be back in no time. Then, once I graduate, I'll be out of your hair," he says without any inflection, telling me he's angry. Instead, I recognize the hurt running rampant in my son.

"You know you don't—"

"I do. This is something I need to do on my own, Dad. I'm grown up now," he tells me. I agree, he is, but he'll always be my son.

His phone beeps. He swipes the screen and taps out a response, then glances at me. "Time to go." He steps up to me, offering me a hug, then I watch my son walk out the door.

I find that I'm not sad at all. I'm proud of the man he's becoming. Strong, independent, and confident.

Heading into my home office, I open my laptop and log into the banking account. Typing in the details I need from the staff document I have saved, I add in the value and hit transfer. The money will hit her account in the next few moments. A smirk lifts the corner of my mouth. She will be mine. Only mine.

I wasn't going to go into the office today, but I have to see her. Perhaps I'll fuck her on the desk. Maybe I'll make her come so hard, Eric will hear and want to watch, and I'll show him how to claim a woman.

I head into the bathroom to get ready for work, my mind on contracting Kristyn to be my escort for the meeting this evening. I'll ensure she's dressed for the occasion. Her beauty will be a deal sealer. Strangely, her stage name fits her perfectly.

Kismet.

Fate.

I've never believed in this shit, but there must be a reason she's walked into my life—into my office. I was the one who found her when she needed a job. Eric told me to do what the fuck I wanted as long as she was something to look at.

The asshole has devoured her and undressed her with his eyes every single day. I don't blame him, though. The clothing she wears is enough to have us all hard as fuck around the office, but I chose her because of her resume.

She has a business degree and is a marketing professional. Having her there to help with advertising has helped business. That makes me wonder what exactly she needs the money she was earning by stripping.

Then I recall her dad. Since I've never met the man, I don't know anything about him. Of course, I know nothing about Kristyn either. The only thing I'm sure of is she wants me as much as I want her.

Once I'm dressed in a tailored charcoal suit and blue button-up, I head out to the car. I don't bother with a tie. Slipping into the driver's seat, I pull out onto the road and head toward the office.

It's quiet when I pull into the parking lot. Not even Eric is in yet. Stalking up the stairs toward the entrance, I step inside, and her perfume immediately assaults me. The scent of lavender fills the space.

When I reach the offices, I find her tapping away at the keyboard. Her eyes snap to mine when I near her.

"Good morning, Mr.—"

"Cut the shit, Kismet. Get me coffee and meet me in my office." I stalk by her without a second glance. I need to steel myself enough to get through the contract I prepared for her. Only then can I look at her and bend her over my desk. The vision is so vivid, I've cemented it in my mind.

She enters my office moments later, but it's too soon. I haven't thought about how I wanted to approach this. When I gave her the offer last night, she agreed, but that was late night angst. She was needy, so was I. Now, in the light of day, I'm not sure she'll go through with it.

"Your coffee, boss," she says quietly, almost shyly, but there's a teasing lilt to the word and I find myself intrigued by her display of submission.

"Thank you. However, if you would like to give me a title, it will be Sir," I offer, and her eyes dart to mine in shock. Her mouth gapes, then closes a second later. Her pouty lips purse, and my dick jolts at the vision.

"I can't...I mean, that's..."

"It turns you on," I tell her, sipping the steaming black liquid. She doesn't deny it. This is something she needs, craves. When I talk to her like that, her body trembles. I've noticed it since the moment she stepped into my office months ago.

"Maybe, but calling you Sir? Are you series?" she utters, scrunching her cute button nose. The act is so innocent, she looks far younger than her twenty-one years. It makes me want to see her dressed in a school uniform with white cotton panties and pigtails.

"You like it dirty," I tell her, settling myself in my

faux leather office chair. "And you like my filthy words." Once again, she doesn't deny it. "Tell me, Kismet," I lean forward, my elbows on top of my cherry wood desk, "did you touch your pretty pussy last night?"

Her cheeks darken with embarrassment. She doesn't respond with words, merely nods her assent. Her body was so pliable, I probably could've sat her on the kitchen table and ate her sweet hole until she gushed all over my face.

"You know, Mr. Kingston, you're vile and crude," she starts, seating herself on the chair. Her left leg crosses over the right, drawing my attention to her smooth calves. Her black heels are about four inches in height, making her legs look longer, even though she's seated.

"Tell me that while calling me by my title," I order, then sit back, waiting for her to refuse. I spread my legs, and watch as her gaze drops to my crotch.

"You're vile and crude," she whispers, lifting her eyes to meet mine once more, "Sir." The word is mumbled with shyness, but it's the most erotic thing I've ever heard.

"Good girl," I praise her with a smile. The air sizzles between us. Electricity I've never felt before shatters the silence between us when she sighs.

"I'll give you what you need, since you've already paid me. However, there will be no sex. Let me make one thing clear." She meets my gaze with a steely glare. *Fuck, she's beautiful.* "I'm not a whore. If you ever offer me money to fuck you, I'll refuse."

Her voice is breathtaking, making my cock hard. It's a rod of metal behind my zipper, all for this beautiful vixen sitting opposite me. Her leg swings over the other, uncrossing them offering me a glimpse of her thighs, though her panties elude me. Frustration is evident as I groan at the sight of her. Seductive, exquisite, perfect.

"I will concede. You're not a whore, but make no mistake, Ms. Marshall, I didn't pay you to fuck me. I gave you that money because I can't see you working in a place like Poison. I want you. I'll fuck you. And when I do, you'll enjoy it, you'll beg me for more, and I'll oblige, because I can never say no to a beautiful woman."

SIX

KRISTYN

When I squirm at his words, he notices. A predatory gaze watches me as if he's about to strike. Every nerve in my body is electrified by his presence, his words. My tongue darts out, licking my lips in a slow motion that has those mocha colored orbs boring into me.

"You want me?"

"I do," he responds with a nod. "Not only because you're beautiful, but because you're a strong, independent woman who makes my cock painfully hard." This time, he smiles. A genuine, wolfish grin that makes him look younger than his forty years. "I'm aching to take you, Kismet," he murmurs, low and gravelly.

Rising, I stalk toward him, feeling more confident

that he not only wants me beside him at the office, but he wants me to sleep with him. If I play it cool, he won't realize I have no idea what I'm doing. That I'm so inexperienced, I'll probably fumble the moment he rips my panties off.

"And when do you think that will be, Mr. Kingston?" I purr his name as I lean over his desk, lifting his silver pen and pressing it to my pouty lips.

"Kristyn." My name is a warning. His eyes dance with electric desire. "I suggest you sign the contract on the printer tray and set it on my desk, then leave my office." There's no confusing his tone. It's dripping with barely restrained need.

"And do you think that's what you really want?"

"Sign the fucking contract," he bites out, his knuckles turning white from his grip on the arm of the chair. I nod slowly and turn to the printer to pick up the said contract. It's one page. Five rules, nothing more. My eyes scan them easily. Using his pen, I scrawl my name on the dotted line.

"There you go, Mr. Kingston." I smirk as I set the page before him. He grabs the pen from my hand, his fingertips brushing along mine, igniting the skin where we made contact. My panties are soaked, the arousal drenching the black lace material.

"Take off your panties," he orders, as if reading my mind.

"What?" My gasp is met with a satisfied smirk. The sinful devil is back, and I have no way of denying him anything. The man looks at me as if I'm his breakfast, lunch, dinner, and decadent dessert.

"You signed the contract. You're obliged to obey everything I ask of you. Now, take off your panties and set them in my hand."

I shuffle the black lace down my thighs and step out of them slowly as my heart thuds wildly at the embarrassment of this situation. I can't stop the blush that heats my cheeks when I notice how wet they are.

He bundles them in his grasp, lifting them to his nose. I watch in awe, shock, and desire as he inhales the scent of me, his eyes fluttering closed in pleasure.

"You smell like you need a good, hard fuck," he tells me. "Do you?" I nod. My throat has closed up and my mouth is as dry as the Sahara Desert. Arid and sandpapery. "Get on my desk, lift that skirt, and show me what's mine."

My body moves.

My mind argues.

My heart leaps into my throat as I bunch my skirt up to my hips. When I settle on his desk, he rolls his chair between my splayed thighs. I've never spread myself so lewdly for a man, but the way his dark eyes regard me, I'm not scared.

"Fuck, that's a pretty little hole," he says as his thumbs spread my smooth lips. "So pink and tight." His words cause me to blush a darker red than before. He leans in, his mouth breathing cool air over my heated flesh, causing me to whimper.

He does it again and again, and my hips rise up, needing him to make contact. But he doesn't. Instead, the man before me teases and taunts, blowing over my puffy entrance. My wetness drips down between my ass cheeks.

"Close your eyes. Just feel," he tells me, and I obey. Taking both my legs, he hangs them over his shoulders and finally allows his mouth to suck on my clit, sending me spiraling through the darkness into euphoria. He doesn't relent. He continues eating my pussy, devouring my flesh, licking and lapping at me.

A soft click sounds in my head, but I can't move as pleasure overrides my body. Every nerve alights, sizzling with electricity as his mouth closes around my clit. His teeth graze it, and he bites down hard, drawing a cry from my very core as my toes curl and body shakes violently.

He moves back an inch, offering me a smirk of delight, his full lips drenched in glistening arousal. "Bend over my desk. I've been dying to do this for months." His order is a feral growl. He's turned into an animal in the space of a few seconds.

When I turn to bend over his cherry oak desk, I gasp. "M-Mr. Pearson." A mumble tumbles from my lips. His blue gaze bores into me as he leans on the doorjamb. Dressed in a charcoal suit and gray shirt, he looks like he's just been to a fancy dinner or a photoshoot with GQ magazine.

"Am I late for breakfast, Levi?" he questions, ignoring me. Mr. Kingston rises behind me, his hands palming the fleshy globes of my ass.

"You just missed breakfast, Pearson." Levi all but pisses on me, his words drenched in possessiveness.

"Too bad. Guess I'll just enjoy the show." Mr. Pearson settles on the chair opposite the desk, his muscled thighs splayed, the large bulge behind his zipper clear. "You look exquisite bent over like that. I must say, Levi, her curves are so utterly tempting. Let me know how tight her slick hole is."

Eric's words are filthy, but I've never been more turned on than I am right now. There's a rip of foil, a soft shuffle, then suddenly, I'm filled to the hilt. Pain sears me as I cry out in agony. Levi is thick, painfully so, and the fact that he just thrust into me, breaking the barrier, has tears forming in my eyes.

He doesn't move for a second, realizing what he's done.

"Please," I beg, needing him to move, or do something. It hurts, but a trickle of pleasure races through my veins.

Levi leans in, his mouth at my ear. "You were a virgin?" I nod, clawing at the desk. "Jesus," he growls in my ear, moving slowly as my body accepts him.

The movement of Levi's hardness knocks the breath from my lungs. Eric grips his cock through his dark slacks as his gaze devours the scene in front of him.

I gasp with every drive Levi pistons into me, my hands slippery as I grasp at the desk. But when Eric

Pearson, the CEO and my boss, pulls his cock from his boxers, I can't keep my eyes from darting to the thick, angry erection.

Beads of arousal seep from the tip as he smirks at my response to his dick. He rises, and my body reels with fear and need. His hand fists my hair harshly, the bite of pain stinging my scalp. I gaze up into irises that remind me of the sky, clear and blue. Gently, ever so gently, he paints his pre-cum on my lips.

"Good girl." He winks, shoving his shaft back into his boxers, then turns to leave. My mouth gapes at his filthy act, but my tongue darts out, licking the saltiness.

"Did you like being my little slut?" Levi wraps my long locks around his hand pulling me backward, and I'm sure they're about to be tugged from the roots. His body leans over me. He's heavy, pressing me into the desk as his cock thickens inside me. "I want you to be my naughty girl," he coos. "Can you do that?"

"Please, Levi, Sir, Mr. Kingston." Words fall unbidden

from my lips as he thrusts into me. The motion is ruthless, but the man himself is lost in his base need.

"Come for me. Give me your fucking pleasure," he bites out, his mouth finding my neck as he sucks the flesh hard. Pain shoots through me as the pleasure of his dick hits that spot inside me.

His hips slam into me. The table protests. I cry out, not caring if anyone hears, when an orgasm, violent and overpowering, wracks through me. Levi shudders behind me, and I realize he joined me in a carnal delight I want again and again.

Our breaths are the only sound in the office. His is ragged and husky, mine gentle and whimpering. His chest vibrates against my back. It's almost soothing, but the flavor on my tongue heats my blood with anger now.

"I thought I was yours?" I whisper, inhaling deeply to calm myself. The arousal Eric coated on my lips like a gloss was degrading, but there was something distinctly filthy that made my orgasm peak. I've never thought about being with two men. Not even thought about it, but with Levi inside me and Mr. Pearson shoving his cock in my face, I am suddenly sure I'd love to be used like that.

What does that make me? A slut. Perhaps.

"You are mine. He knows never to come near you, unless I'm there." Levi's husky tone whispers over my flesh. It tickles the skin on my neck now sheened in sweat from our fucking.

"And you'll allow him to use me, if you so see fit?" I ask as he rises, allowing me up. I watch him rip the condom off and dispose of it in his trashcan. His cock, even soft, is thick and long. I've never felt so full, so claimed, than I did when Levi drove into my body. My thin vibrator is nothing compared to this man.

"No man will come near this pretty pussy." He cups me between my legs, his palm pressing hard on my clit. "Are you going to be a naughty slut and come for me again?" he murmurs, his lips planting a kiss on mine. My head drops back as he dips two fingers into my aching hole. I'm sore, deliciously so.

He pumps both digits into me, faster, harder, so ferocious and violent, but so beautifully intoxicating. My knees buckle. My hands claw at him for more...for less. I'm not sure what I need, but Levi does.

"You're mine. All fucking mine. Do you understand me? This hole is made for my dick." He moves his free hand to my ass, finding the puckered entrance. One finger teases me there, sending ripples of anxiety and desire racing through me. "This hole right here, is mine too."

My gaze snaps open to meet his. "Levi."

"And this mouth, those pouty lips, are mine to fuck, to kiss, to devour. Every inch of your body is mine."

I nod, my mind on the pressure he's putting on my clit and ass. I'm flying. Soaring through the clouds as he bites my shoulder, his teeth sharp and animalistic as I claw at him. I'm on the peak. I need this. I want it. His digit slips into the tight entrance I've never had penetrated as two fingers inside my pussy rub against the soft spot that turns me inside out. My body leaps into the abyss as euphoria overtakes me.

Fireworks go off behind my eyelids, and I soak his hand. My body shudders wildly as my legs give out. I'm being held up by his hands inside me. I'm gushing. It feels as if I'm peeing, but it's not. I've only ever read about this. About an orgasm so strong, a woman can squirt.

"I...I...oh god." My voice is otherworldly. I'm not even sure it's me speaking. He doesn't move. I'm practically climbing him. My toes are curled so hard, they ache. My limbs are jelly.

When I open my eyes, coming down from the high, I find a handsome smirking face inches from mine.

"You're a naughty little girl," he murmurs in my ear. "Did it turn you on? Having Pearson here while I was deep inside you?"

He removes his fingers from my body and lifts them to paint my arousal on my lips. Then, he gently kisses me, his tongue lapping at my flavor on my mouth.

"Maybe," I respond. "But I want to be yours." It's a confession that stills him for a moment. Tipping my head to the side, I regard him earnestly.

SEVEN

LEVI

"You are mine, but I'll use you however I see fit." Settling in the chair, I sit back and watch her mind work through everything that's happened. I didn't mean to fuck her right here, but she looked too beautiful.

"And if I don't agree to it?" Her question is filled with curiosity, yet her expression tells me there's desire trickling through her. She enjoyed the fact that Eric walked in here and saw her being fucked. Maybe she wants a threesome. Who knows.

"You can't refuse me now, baby girl," I tell her. "Tonight, you'll meet me at my house. There's a dinner I'm having with a client and you'll be my arm candy for the evening."

"Arm candy?" she retorts, fire blazing in her eyes.

"You'll be my plus one. And I have a dress for you to wear, so don't go buying anything with the money I gave you."

She sighs, nods, and offers a smile. "Fine. But don't ever call me arm candy."

"Of course, baby girl. I need more coffee." I push the mug over to her. "This one is cold."

She lifts the cup and leaves my office with an extra sway in her hips. Just then, Trevor and Eric stalk through the door.

"If you're going to fuck in your office, can you keep it down?" Trevor chirps. He's wearing those goddamn flip flops again. Bright fucking green.

"If you're going to wear a suit, you should get some proper fucking shoes," I retort.

The man is strange, but he's good at what he does. He's an asset to FFF, and I wouldn't want to work with anyone else. We've come together as partners and built this from the ground up. I trust them with millions of my own money, and I don't do that easily.

"Fuck you, Kingston," he bites back, lifting one sandaled foot and placing it over the opposite knee.

"Listen, you fuck when and where you want, just don't let our clients hear," Eric says.

"And you? What young toy are you banging?" I taunt, earning me the bird. "Listen, this new contract with Sanders needs to be finalized. I have a meeting tonight that will be bringing in another ten million, so I'll need Trevor working on the numbers when I get in tomorrow morning."

Both men nod.

"It's done." Trevor smirks. Pushing out of the chair, he drops a thick folder on my desk. "Read through it, sign it, and get it back to me."

Opening the manila folder, I find all the documents I need to get signed tonight at my meeting. "You're a lifesaver, Trev." I glance up at him.

"I know," he quips, and heads out the door. "I'm going to brunch, and I might not be back till tomorrow," he informs us with a satisfied, yet cheesy grin, then he's gone.

"Asshole," I chuckle.

"So," Eric starts, "you and our office assistant?"

"Yeah." I meet his blue eyes as he stares at me as if considering what to say next. "Listen, this isn't going—"

"I don't give a shit who you're banging, Kingston. She's hot. Perhaps we can all play together. Just keep her quiet. As much as I love hearing her cute little squeals, I can't be sitting in a meeting with a hard-on from your porn show."

"You're a dick, Pearson."

He shrugs it off with a guffaw. We both know it's true. He can't deny it.

"I can't wait for the day when a pretty little toy has you all wound up over her," I inform him with a smirk.

"Nah. You know I like to fuck 'em and leave 'em, no

need in getting feelings involved."

"Oh, I know. I'm still waiting on the day." Eric is going to get himself all torn up over one of his conquests; it's only a matter of time.

EIGHT

KRISTYN

His house is decadent. It's triple the size of the home I share with my dad. I feel out of my depth as I wander around the modern rooms. I'm still in my work clothes, but I follow Levi's directions, finding the bedroom he told me about.

When I step inside, I can't stifle a gasp. This is purely exquisite. Floor-to-ceiling windows. A small balcony overlooking the ocean. I move toward the doors and slide them open. The fresh air is intoxicating as I inhale it. The view is spectacular, which only hurts my heart. I wish my dad could see how beautiful this is.

Shaking the sadness from my mind, I head back inside and take in the king-sized bed with a navy-blue comforter which looks more expensive than anything I own. There are four posts on either corner, and I picture myself being bound by Mr. Kingston while he devours every inch of my body.

Once more, I'm tempted to touch myself, but his orders were clear. I'm meant to change into the lingerie on the bed and wait for him in the living room.

The soft silk corset and panties are elegant, yet so beautifully sexy. They're nothing like I imagined. When he told me what he wanted, I figured he was a filthy old man. This is utterly luxurious.

My mind is lost in thought when my phone pings from my purse. I pull it out and unlock the screen to find a message from Levi.

I trust you like the gift. I can't wait to see those curves decked in silk.

Reading the message again and again, I find a happy smile curving my lips. I may have a bigger bank account because I agreed to this, but my heart has a different idea. I'm enjoying Levi's games, his filthy words, but I can't allow myself to fall.

This is temporary, and I don't want more heartache in my life. There's only so much I can handle. Unzipping my skirt, I make quick work of changing into the panties. Once they're snug around my hips, I manage to get the corset on and tied. Thankfully, it's easier than I envisioned. When I take a quick glance in the mirror, I don't recognize the woman staring back at me.

"Perfect," a deep voice comes from the doorway, causing me to yelp with fright. My head spins, finding Levi leaning against the doorjamb. His arms are folded across his chest, his tie is gone, and the shirt he's wearing is unbuttoned just enough to tease me with a glimpse of his smooth, tanned skin.

His dark hair is messy. It stands in every direction, and I wonder how many times he's raked his fingers through it.

"How was the rest of your meeting?" I turn to him, offering him a full view of my body. His gaze roves over me, from my long chestnut waves down to the suede open-toe heels I'm wearing. The bright pink on my toes pops against the dark material of my shoe.

His tongue darts out, licking at his full lips. When his eyes land on mine once more, he smirks. "You look good enough to eat," he says, ignoring my question. "When I come home, I don't want to talk work. When I'm alone with you, it's just us—your beautiful body either beneath mine, over mine, or against mine. Either way, when we're in this house, I'll be fucking you anywhere I like."

"What about your son?" I question easily. The story I've heard is Levi's wife died years ago, and ever since, he's been alone, raising Ethan, his eighteen-year-old son. I wonder if this whole ruse is just for him to have company. As soon as I think it, I know it's a lie. This man could have any woman. Why me?

"He's away on a school trip. It's just us, my sweet

Kismet," he quips. Those dark eyes meet mine in a searing gaze. The way he's looking at me, I'm sure dinner will be delayed.

"And I'm meant to be your babysitter?" I tease, stalking closer to him, finding confidence from the power I hold over him. In the office, he's the boss, but in here, I have a feeling I can exert some of my power.

"Darling, the only thing you'll be sitting is my cock." He grips my hips, tugging me harshly against his solid frame. His body is deliciously toned, the muscles flexing under the material of his shirt. "Tonight, you'll be my escort to a business meeting. You'll wear the silver dress hanging in the walk-in closet. Leave the lingerie under. I'll be tearing it all off when we get back, then I'll fuck you 'til you can't stand."

Smirking, he turns, leaving me gaping at his broad shoulders. My body eagerly responds to his alpha display. I want Levi. I really do. What worries me is what happens when he's tired of me.

Sighing, I head toward the closet and find the dress in question. It's sleek, silky, and has a beautiful neckline embroidered with diamante that shimmer under the low lights in the closet. There are many more dresses hanging on the silver rails, but this one is definitely elegant and beautiful.

I take my time slipping into the delicate material, which seems to hug my curves. The feminine cut is low at the back with a scoop neck that shows just enough cleavage for a business dinner, but also to taunt Levi with.

Smiling at my reflection, I shut the door and head out of the bedroom. When I hear soft music playing downstairs, I follow the sound, which leads me to the living room where Levi is standing in a black suit tailored to his frame.

"I'm ready," I utter almost shyly.

He spins on his heel, finding me at the entrance to the large room. His eyes widen, and I suddenly feel nervous at the way he's regarding me.

"You are perfection, you know that?" He closes the distance between us, pulling me into his arms. Gently, his lips plant a soft kiss on my head. "And you're all mine."

I smile at the sweetness of the moment. This man will be my undoing.

NINE

LEVI

THE RESTAURANT IS FULL OF MEN IN SUITS WITH beautiful women in the latest designer clothes draped over them. Dresses so beautiful, any man would be completely intoxicated by the elegance in the room.

When we reach the table, the hostess sets the menus down. I pull out Kristyn's chair, ensuring she's seated beside me. I want her close for what I have in mind. This is a little test to see how much she's willing to put up with.

The waiter appears, takes our drinks order, and leaves. I'm staring at the menu when Brent arrives with a woman who's not his wife clinging to him like a second skin. Her blonde hair and big green eyes are made up for a night out on the town.

She's dressed like a common whore in a dress so

short, I'm sure I catch a glimpse of her cunt beneath the hemline. It wouldn't surprise me if she weren't wearing any panties. Her lips are fake, blown up by Botox. She's fake, plastic—someone Pearson would love to stick his dick in.

"Levi," Brent smirks. "This is Gigi." She smiles, shaking my hand.

"This is Kristyn," I introduce my girl. I'm proud to be beside her. Knowing she's as filthy as she is elegant. I love a naughty woman, but when she's out in public, she'll dress like a lady. However, when I get her alone, that's another story.

"Nice to meet you, Mr. Masterson." Kristyn smiles, shaking his hand, and I can't help noticing the way he leers at her. Knowing this in one of the last shipments we'll be doing for him is the only reason I'm not knocking him out.

"It's my pleasure, sweet thing," he chuckles, holding onto her hand for a little too long.

I've known him most of my working career, and he's been a client I depend on. He pays on time and doesn't give me too much shit.

The only thing I don't like is how he cheats on his wife. She's a stunner, and the fact that he's out with this doll on his arm frustrates me to no end.

"Shall we get some drinks?" he asks Gigi when the waiter appears with the wine I ordered. The young man opens the bottle with a flourish and fills our glasses after I agree on the taste.

"I want something pink and fruity." Gigi giggles, and I wonder how old she really is.

Brent orders, and the waiter leaves us. He turns his attention on me. "So, there are two shipments coming in. I need them both handled by Four Fathers," he tells me.

"We can certainly do that. Give me the deadlines, locations, and I can have the invoice sent out to you first thing in the morning."

He nods with a satisfied smile.

"There's something else I need your help with." I knew this was coming. Brent is a dealer. He loves the challenge of making the most asinine deals with men and then coming to me for help. It doesn't make a difference what it is.

I, however, am able to give him the legal advice he normally needs when things go awry. My father's insistence at getting an education when I was younger has ensured I'm geared to run an empire on my own.

"Anything for you, Brent." I lift my glass as their drinks arrive. While they're talking to our server, my hand snakes over Kristyn's thigh, squeezing her toned leg while chatting with Masterson. There's a soft whimper from my left, and I can't help smirking against my glass.

My fingers trail up 'til I find her smooth skin where the material is cut. I chose this dress for a reason, and this is why. My fingers move deftly over the lace and satin of her panties, stroking her gently, applying pressure to her clit when I feel she needs it.

"I'm glad I can count on you, Levi. Your father was a great man and he's trained you well," he informs me, and I nod.

"Thank you. He was a bastard at times," I tell him as my fingers snake their way under her panties. Her hand grips mine, attempting to tug it away, but she's not strong enough. I cast a glance over at her while Brent and Gigi decide on dinner. "But he was good at teaching me exactly what is needed to run a successful business."

"Even though you don't need the money," Brent chuckles.

"You're right," I agree. I don't need the money. My father left enough for me to live off until I breathe my final breath.

The slick juices dripping over my fingers cause my cock to throb in time with my heart beat. The thudding is painful, but I don't stop taunting my little Kismet as she bites her plump lower lip.

"I...I need the restroom," Kristyn mumbles against

me. Her face is flushed, beautiful and rosy. She's exquisite as she sits on the brink of an orgasm.

"Right now?" I quip, dipping two fingers into her and feeling her pulse wildly around them. Her body is so close. All she needs is one tiny little push and she'll be freefalling at my touch. Controlling a woman's orgasm is my drug, and watching Kristyn unravel for me is my addiction.

"Please," she whimpers when I add a third finger into her sopping little hole. My hand pumps her harder, faster, and her eyes glaze over as her cunt clamps down hard, sucking me into her body as an orgasm rips through her.

One tiny mewl is all I get, and I know she's perfect. There's something about a woman coming in public and managing to keep her composure.

"Okay, darling." I smirk, pulling my fingers from her, and bring them to my mouth to taste her sweetness. They glisten as I devour her flavor.

"Levi, will you be able to help out a friend of mine

with a contract as well?" Brent asks as Kristyn races to the ladies' room. I nod without missing a beat.

"Of course," I tell him. "The more the merrier. Tell me more." I lean in, feigning interest. The only thing on my mind is how beautifully my little tease came all over my fingers.

"Perfect. I'll have him send over his requirements in the morning. He's one of my oldest friends. A man with more money than God." Brent chuckles, his arm looping around Gigi's neck as he tugs her into his hold.

When Kristyn returns, she's not as flushed, but her eyes still give away the desire swirling throughout her pretty little body.

"You okay, sweetheart?" I ask, earning a glare.

Tonight will be fun.

TEN

KRISTYN

THE DINNER IS THE LAST THING ON MY MIND. EACH time Mr. Masterson asks me a question, I'm jarred because I'm not listening. His date is nothing more than eye candy, but even though she's dressed provocatively, Levi hasn't given a second glance.

Each time she speaks, I can feel the frustration emanating from beside me. Levi hasn't tried to taunt me again, but his hand hasn't left my thigh either. There's a possessiveness in his grip, and I welcome it more than I think I should.

"That's it then." Brent rises, attempting to button his jacket over a rounding stomach. He's easily in his early fifties, which begs the question of how Gigi, who looks like she just graduated high school, can be with a man like that. Then I notice his wallet as he tugs it from his slacks. The thick wad of cash is the answer to my inner query.

"It's been good seeing you again, Brent." Levi rises, finally releasing my leg from the confines of his large hand.

Brent nods. "And you." The men shake, and Mr. Masterson's ogling gaze falls to me once more. "It was a pleasure meeting you, sweetheart." He offers me a smirk, which I can only respond to with a smile. Words evade me as this man who's old enough to be my father, or grandfather actually, looks at me like he wants to rip my dress off.

The thought sickens me when he takes my hand in his and plants a kiss on my knuckles. Once he leaves, Levi and I are alone again, and I'm even more aware of him. The wine I gulped has heated my skin and my stomach tumbles in anticipation of what's to come.

Since it's only ten o'clock, I know there's so much more Levi wants to do tonight. He doesn't have to voice it, but it's there in his eyes when our gazes lock.

"Sorry it took so long," he apologizes. There's a sincerity to him at times, but there is also a calloused harshness where I can see he's hiding emotion. I understand closing yourself off when you lose someone you love, and it's clear Levi has done that over the years.

"It's okay. I can't believe you did what you did," I tell him, earning a haughty chuckle. The sound is deep and rumbles low in his chest.

"Why? Didn't you enjoy it?" he quips. His confidence is stifling at times. He wears it like a cologne. But I would be lying if I said I didn't want it.

"I-I mean—"

"Don't lie to me, Kismet," he warns. His body is so close to mine, caging me into the corner of the booth where his hand grips my thigh once more. "I don't like liars. I take them, spank their pretty little asses, then fuck their tight little pussies until they're squirming, and you know what I do after?" He doesn't wait for me to respond before continuing with more filthy promises that have my panties drenched and clit tingling. "I make them lick all those sweet juices from my dick. I do that so they can learn to keep those plump lips closed and not be dishonest about their needs."

"You're utterly filthy," I bite out in response, but the way I'm trembling, he can tell it's not from fear. I'm turned on. I'm so wet, he could probably push his fist inside me easily.

"And you wouldn't have it any other way. I bet those pretty panties are drenched. I can smell you, little Kismet. If I took that scrap of material and licked it, I know you'd be even more turned on."

"Levi, we should go," I murmur, my voice dropping into a whisper that is so quiet, I'm not sure he heard me. His gaze flickers and his mouth curls into a smirk.

"Take this," he says, offering me a handkerchief from his pocket. "And put it between your legs. Right now." His order is clear. Snatching the material from him, I move it under the tablecloth and position it between my thighs. "Press hard against your pussy," he growls like a goddamn caveman.

"This is ridic—"

"I didn't ask you to speak. You're to obey me. Remember the rules, Kristyn, or you'll be punished severely."

"What? Are you going to spank me?" I retort hotly. His face changes into something dark and devilish. There's a sinister, yet sinful glimmer in his dark eyes, and I wonder if I just unlocked a devil I'd rather have hidden away.

"I'd do that and so much more. Hand me the handkerchief," he commands. His presence alone is breathtaking, but when he's in his element, being domineering, that's when he's a king.

I hand him the soaked material, and he lifts it to his face, inhaling my scent. Something about the way he does it, so wrong and taboo, makes me ache. My body craves what he offers.

All my life, I've been the good girl. I never did anything to jeopardize my schooling, my work, or my life, but with Levi, I want to break all the rules. He's dangerous—not only to my body, but my heart.

"We're leaving," he bites out. When he slips from the booth, he offers his hand to help me out. My dress falls perfectly closed, covering my intimate areas he had on display under the table moments ago.

As we head for the exit, women, men, and couples all watch him, their eyes glued to the man who commands it. He doesn't offer them a second glance, but they look at him as if he's royalty, and I find myself wonder if he really is. How much do I know about Levi Kingston?

"Get out of your pretty little head, baby girl," he tells me with that husky, whiskey-laden tone. It sounds as smoky as the alcohol he's been drinking.

"What do you mean?"

He stops suddenly, halting on the sidewalk where we

almost crash into other couples walking hand in hand. From a distance, we look like them, but upon closer inspection, we're nothing alike. "You think too much," he offers.

"And why is that so bad?"

"Because, baby girl, there's so much more of a world out there when you stop thinking so much." He leans in, his lips brushing against my ear. "Come." He laces his fingers through mine, tugging me toward the ocean. We can walk there, but I've never been anywhere close to the pier at night.

My father's always been one to watch me like a hawk. Now that I have freedom, I'm unsure of what to do with it. Levi seems to have more of a free spirit than I do, and he's twice my age. That saddens me somewhat. I'm not like other twenty-one-year-olds. I don't go out clubbing; I look after my father.

Moments later, we're on the pier, looking out over the blackened ocean as it crashes wildly against the shore, in the same way Levi crashed into my life. Like a wave knocking my feet from under me, he's slowly dragging me into his depths, and I'm afraid I'll drown in him.

"It's beautiful," I say, focusing on the cresting tide. The darkness swallows us as we step off the pier onto the sand. Levi holds my hand so I can slip off my shoes.

He leads me closer to the water, our feet on the cool, wet beach. My skin tingles from the chilly water, but it does nothing to quell the heat Levi ignites within me. And that scares me more than anything else.

ELEVEN

LEVI

SHE SILENTLY WATCHES THE WAVES, HER HAND gripping mine almost painfully. Something about this girl changes me. She doesn't back down from a challenge, but she has a fragility that makes me want to protect her.

Not because I feel she's mine, but because she has an innocence I want to nurture. I may give Eric grief for choosing younger, plastic dolls to fuck, but those are the innocent ones who will give you their all. And I have a feeling Kristyn will do that with me.

The dark waves beat against the shore, attacking it with vengeance, as if telling me I'm fucking up. I want this girl. I want to fuck her, hurt her, make her cry—and I want her to crave me doing those things. I know deep down she enjoys darker delights, but it's that tiny flame inside her that holds me back.

Suddenly, she rips her hand from my grasp, reaches for the hem of her dress, and peels it off, leaving me with the view of her black lingerie. "Time to let go," she giggles, racing toward the water.

Her body hits the chilly waves, her skin glistening in the low light of the moon and a few strobe lights from the bars and clubs on the strip. Thankfully, there's no one else around. If any other man laid eyes on her right now, I'd probably beat them to death.

Those chestnut waves that were styled perfectly only moments ago are loose, drenched in the salty water. Her smooth skin taunts me with droplets of water shimmering like diamonds. A precious jewel.

Her giggles echo back to me. "Hey, come join me, Mr. Kingston." She smiles.

Pulling off my tie, I drop it on the sand. My shirt follows, along with my slacks and socks. I'm left in only a pair of boxers as I wade into the depths.

Gentle rolling waves attack me. I grip her hips when I reach her, pulling her curvy frame against me. She fits into my every nook. "You called, little Kismet?" I growl into her ear, causing a tremble to shoot through her.

"Levi." The soft murmur of my name on her lips makes my cock throb against her pert little ass. It hardens painfully, wanting to slide inside her—to claim her. My hands grip her ass cheeks, lifting her against me. Her long, lithe legs wrap around my waist while her arms twine around my neck.

"I'm going to do things to your body right here. I want to hear you scream over the crash of the waves." I shove my boxers down my thighs with one hand and my cock juts out, pressing against her panty-clad entrance. "Move your panties. I want inside you," I bite out through clenched teeth.

Her hands move swiftly, obeying my order like a good girl should. Rolling my hips, I inch into her tight heat, savoring each and every whimper she allows to escape. Her head drops back and her eyes flutter closed as I thrust deeper, fully seating myself in her pussy.

"Oh god," she whimpers, her nails clawing at my shoulders as she begins to bounce along with the waves. Our bodies are jostled, but we're connected so deeply, nothing breaks us apart.

It's been a long time since I've felt anything more than lust for a woman, but with Kristyn, I find affection creeping in. It's a gentle nudge each time I'm with her.

"Ride me. I want to feel you take control," I tell her.

Those blue gems pierce me when she snaps them my way. Using her legs and hands, she lifts herself, then eases down my shaft. Again, and again. My cock throbs with every movement of her slick walls as they pulse and flutter.

"Do you like me fucking you, Kismet?"

"I do," she confesses, her pearly whites biting down on her lower lip. Her pupils dilate as she watches me intently while taking my dick inside her. My fingers trail to the crack of her pretty ass, nudging her panties to the side. My index finger taunts the tight hole, circling it, teasing it. "I...I...oh..." she whimpers as it dips into her.

"You're so tight, I bet my cock would rip you apart," I chuckle. Her tits bounce in front of me, and my mouth finds one nipple. Latching on, I bite down hard while fingering her asshole as she rides me faster.

"I'm going to—"

She cries out, but can't finish the sentence when I insert a second digit. The shudder of her body is the only evidence that an orgasm has just coursed through her because her eyes are locked on mine. I've been with many women over the years, but having her look directly at me as she unravels is the most beautiful thing I've ever seen.

"Levi," she mumbles again, dropping her head into the crook of my neck.

"I'm going to fuck you now, baby girl," I warn as I wade out of the deep water and press her against one of the wooden pillars of the pier.

With her back flush against it, I pull out slowly, then slam back into her cunt. Her screams echo around me as I fuck her mercilessly. I'm violent, rough, but the arousal dripping from her tells me she's loving it.

My hand grips her neck, my mouth crashes down on the smooth, supple swell of her breast, and I bite down hard, sucking the flesh into my mouth, my teeth surely close to breaking skin.

Her body convulses and her cunt tightens, sucking me deeper inside. Her mewls and whimpers are music to my ears as I drive myself so deep, I'm sure I'm hitting her womb. A thought hits me violently. I want her pregnant with my baby.

I want her swelling with my seed.

Again, and again, my hips crash into hers. Her nails rake through my hair, over my neck and shoulders, until I feel her draw blood. My release shoots through me, and I empty myself inside her.

We still for a moment, my breathing ragged, sweat glistening on both our bodies. Kristyn is still trembling. A gentle vibration races through her body as the pleasure slowly subsides.

"You're a good girl, Kismet," I coo into her ear, planting kisses along her collarbone and the curve of her neck. When I reach her ear, I tug it into my mouth, suckling the flesh which is free of any earrings. Her flavor is sweet, alluring, and I want to taste every inch of her body. I want her to yearn for my tongue, my fingers, and ultimately, I want her to be a slut for my cock.

"You make me feel things," she whispers. It's so quiet, I almost miss it. Almost. I don't respond. Instead, I let her down and help her back into the dress she discarded on the beach.

Once we're dressed, we make our way up toward the road and back to the restaurant where my car is parked.

The silence surrounding us is stifling.

You make me feel things.

Her words echo in my brain. They knock around in my chest, attempting to grip my heart. I locked it away so long ago, I forgot I have one.

I can't fall for this girl.

She's merely entertainment for the time being. There's one way to cure this stupidity, and that's to share her with a friend. To watch her fuck someone else will ensure I focus on what I'm doing with her: playtime.

The drive is quiet, but I hear her.

It's as if she's talking to me with all those thoughts running rampant in her mind.

I didn't want her to feel anything more than pleasure. It's only our first night. What happens at the end of the thirty days?

I have to put a stop to this.

"Are you angry with me?" she asks from the passenger seat. Her tentative tone is jarring, like a child who's been admonished by her parents.

"No, of course not. I'm taking you home. I'll see you

tomorrow." I smile, but it's fake. I'm not happy to be taking her home, but I need to.

When we finally pull up to the house, I exit the car and round to her side. Helping her out, I wait a moment before pulling her in for a kiss goodnight.

"You can be romantic when you try hard enough," she teases. The tension leaves my shoulders for a moment as I chuckle at her words.

"Don't get used to it. Tomorrow, I'm fucking you on my desk."

Last night, I dreamed of her. Her body, those lips, eyes, tits—everything about this woman has caught me unaware.

A knock on my office door tells me she's on the other side. My cock thickens, my heart thuds wildly, and I bite back a groan as an image of her on my desk assaults me.

"Come inside."

She does, her hips swaying as she heads toward my desk. The door closes behind her, sequestering us from everyone else in the building. It's just us. Her sweet perfume makes me rise from my seat. My hands are on her hips, pulling her closer, needing every inch of my body against hers. I want to see her cheeks flush, her lips part on a moan, and I want her nails digging into my scalp as I make her come all over my face.

"Bend over my desk and hitch up your skirt. I want to take you right now."

"Levi." It's a warning, but my name on her lips only fuels my need.

"Do it." The order is clear. Do not deny me what I want. Fucking her like this will stop my feelings from turning into something more—something I'm not capable of giving her. Her pupils dilate as desire courses through her, sending a shiver over her body.

"I wanted to—"

"I didn't ask you to speak. I need to fuck you. If you

can't obey an order, then get the fuck out of my office, Kristyn," I utter in frustration. My emotions are in turmoil right now. "I just...I need this."

Her gaze darkens with confusion. I expect a sassy retort, but she doesn't say anything for a long while. We stare at each other in silence, wordless promises and affections hanging between us.

Finally, she moves, glances over her shoulder at me, and murmurs, "We shouldn't be doing this," with flushed cheeks and pouty lips. Her big eyes, the color of the ocean, peek at me from over her shoulder. The sleek gray skirt bunched over her hips and fleshy globes of her ass are pointed right at me.

"We shouldn't have done it the first, second, or third time, but that didn't stop us. Did it?" I quip as I palm her flesh. My voice drips with hunger for this woman—this girl who's half my age. Granted, not all twenty-somethings make me hard as steel when they walk into my office.

Opening her to my gaze, I lean in to find a sweet, wet spot of arousal on her pastel blue panties. "Did you wear these for me?" I grip the material with my thumbs and tug them over her hips, down her long slender legs. Her scent is intoxicating. My office is going to smell of fucking when I'm done, but I don't give a shit.

"Don't flatter yourself, Mr. Kingston," she retorts.

Lifting my hand, I rain down a swat on her ass, left, right, then down her thighs until her knees buckle. The red markings have my cock hardening further. I'm no longer semi-aroused. Now, I'm ready to fuck her into next year while she comes all over my thick shaft.

"Please, Sir," she mumbles as she claws my desktop, trying to find purchase.

Ignoring her, I splay her beautiful ass once more. Both holes open to me—to anything I want to do to her body. I lean in, running my nose up her inner thigh, just missing her core.

Mimicking the action on her left leg, I can't help

the smirk that curls my lips when she whimpers. The glistening hole of her cunt is needy and ready for me. My tongue darts out, lapping at her smooth lips, causing her to cry out my name.

"If you don't shut up, Eric will be stalking in here to see what's going on," I grunt out through clenched teeth. I know he's in a meeting with a client and won't bother if my office door is closed, but she stays silent, heeding my warning.

Rising, I take the shredded panties and stuff them into her mouth. Her eyes are wide with shock and indignation, but I merely offer her a shrug before moving behind her once more and kneeling between her thighs. With another long lap at her holes, I tease the puckered one with my tongue. Her response is a muffled mewl.

My fingers move to her pussy. I dip two inside her, feeling her pulse around them. Her slick heat, tight and warm, taunts me and my cock. I continue fucking her slowly, my thumb circling her clit, sending her spiraling.

Her legs shake, shuddering as she cries out once more when her orgasm shatters through her. Taking both fingers, I trail them up to her tight hole and finger it open. She's still coming down from her high when I slip into her ass.

Giving her no time to recover, I reach for her hardened clit with my other hand and tweak it until she's unraveling on my desk once more. Sweet, musky juices drip from her, and I lap them up like a starving man.

Pulling my fingers from her, I shove my slacks down along with my boxer briefs. My shaft juts out toward her, needing to drive into her. With one hand, I fist my cock, teasing it up and down her slit, the tip glistening with our mingled arousal.

Without warning, I grip her hips and plunge balls-deep inside her tight cunt. She whimpers, and I growl low in my chest as she holds onto the desk. My hips leave her as I pull back, then slam back into her, fucking her into the wooden top.

My fingers on her hips pin her down as I move faster. She's tight, so fucking tight, squeezing my cock inside her. I rain down a swat on either cheek, watching her body pulse from the assault. Her puckered hole is mine. I lean in and spit on it, working two fingers inside while keeping rhythm of my cock in her cunt.

Our bodies slam into each other as I take her.

Kismet.

She's my fate.

My balls draw up as another release tenses her from the tips of her toes up to ends of her fingers. She cries out into the material, and I join her, emptying myself inside her.

TWELVE

KRISTYN

IT'S BEEN A WEEK.

Well, almost ten days to be exact.

Each night, I go to Levi's house. Every time I'm there, we fuck. He loses himself inside me, and I lose my heart to him. I should stop it. I'm going to get hurt and there's nothing I can do because I feel more for him than I should. I see the pain in his eyes when he looks at me. It's clear. He's warring with his emotions too. But neither of us puts a stop to what we're doing.

As if we're both addicts. I want him more than I should. My dreams are haunted by him, but it's my heart that's slowly warming to his brand of dirty. His words, his actions—everything about him is wrong for me.

Pushing open the door to his house, I step inside,

finding it silent. Normally, he has music playing when I arrive, but tonight, there's nothing. It's deafening. Inching my way through the foyer, I find him in the kitchen. He's dressed in a pair of sweats and nothing else.

I finished up work late because Eric wanted the early morning meeting's minutes typed up, but now that I'm here, the stress of the work day disappears.

"Baby girl." He smiles, finding me in the doorway. He makes his way over, planting a kiss on my cheek. The smell of whiskey on his breath is enough to tell me there's something very wrong.

"Are you okay?"

He nods. Since he wasn't at work today, I figured he may be sick, but then he messaged me to come over, so here I am.

"I mean, you weren't at work," I continue when he doesn't say anything. Setting my purse on the table, I settle on the chair, watching him move about the kitchen making something that smells delicious. "I didn't know you cooked."

"Not since... it's something that I used to do with...," he utters finally his words tapering into silence and I know he's thinking about his wife.

Okay. It's like I'm having an out of body experience. Normally, he's on me in seconds, ripping at my clothes, wanting me naked. This is more than strange, it's scary.

"So, I—"

"Take off your clothes. Sit on the table. Don't speak." His words are colder than normal. Almost as if it's someone else in Levi's body.

I shuffle to my feet and unzip my skirt, allowing it to fall to the floor. My blouse is the next to pool at my feet. I'm about to settle on the table when he turns around to glare at me.

"All your clothes. I want you naked."

His short, brusque sentences jar me. Even though he can be an asshole, this is on a whole other level. But for some reason, I don't leave. I don't walk out on him. He's hurting. When I stare into those dark eyes, I see the pain etched in them so deeply, it grips my heart.

Once my panties are on the floor, I perch myself on the kitchen table. The dark sky is filled with stars that twinkle on the other side of the window. I focus on those, wondering if I'm doing the right thing. Even though I know Levi's wife is no longer alive, I feel as if I'm cheating with a married man because of the way he's looking at me right now.

In this moment I feel most like the *other woman.* Perhaps he doesn't mean to do it, but my heart aches in my chest realizing that maybe he's still in love with her and I'm only a distraction.

"Open your legs. Finger your pretty cunt," he growls, turning off the stove. He stalks toward the table as if he's about to attack me, but he doesn't. His body looms over me as he watches my hand snake down my flat stomach to find my pussy.

I'm already wet. My finger dips inside, finding the

arousal Levi elicits from my body with his harsh words. I'm broken, shattered for this man, and all my cracks are filled with him.

As much as I want to deny it, I'm falling into his abyss, and there's no way out.

"Levi, I—"

He grips my hand, shoves it away, and spanks my pussy so hard, I cry out in shock.

"I told you not to speak," he warns, leaning in closer. He runs his nose along my inner thigh until he reaches the apex. When he rises, he rains down another swat on my tingling lips. Tears spring to my eyes as he continues slapping my tits, pussy, and inner thighs. They turn bright red before he finally stops.

"You're so beautiful, aren't you?" he questions.

I don't answer, because I'm not sure I am. Yes, I'm pretty, I guess, but no one has ever called me beautiful. He massages my tender skin, but doesn't make a move to touch my pussy. He laps his tongue over my breasts, nipples, and thighs. Small bruises dot my flesh where he's bitten me while we've had sex, and I wear them proudly.

"You're mine, and so fucking beautiful it hurts me."

His words sting. Not painfully, but they make my heart hurt over the fact that he can't love me—especially since I know I love him. I've fallen for a man whose heart is so firmly locked away, I don't think I'll ever have access to it. I'm stupid for believing he could feel something. I'm nothing more than a whore who's been paid to fuck him.

"Get out of your head, Kristyn," he utters against my knee. Baring his teeth down on the skin, he bites as much as he can against the bone, causing me to whimper. "Is your pretty pussy wet for me?"

"Yes," I whisper, ashamed his spanking turned me on. I'm needy once more, wanting him to use me. I wish he would break me so I don't feel what I do for him. I wish I could hate him, feel anger toward him, but I don't.

In a swift move, he shoves his sweats down, his cock jutting, thick and angry, from between his thighs. The veins protrude from the shaft, causing it to look scary. He fists it, stroking up and down my nether lips, coating himself in my arousal.

A whimper falls from my lips when he slaps my clit with the tip of his cock. He doesn't waste another minute before sliding into me. I watch as his body connects with mine. I avoid looking at his face so I don't see the pain in his expression.

There's something different about this.

There's more emotion between us in this moment than there has been since we started this strange relationship. He's deep inside me now, hitting my cervix with every thrust. His hips fit between my thighs. His thumb circles my clit, causing my pussy to tighten around him, pulsing in pleasure.

"I want your ass tonight," he grits out between clenched teeth, his jaw ticking. The thought has me spiraling. Even though he's fingered me there, he's never pushed for anal. Now he wants it, and I'm scared.

Without warning, he pulls out and grips my hips, tugging me off the table. I'm bent over and my legs are spread before I have time to fathom what's happened. His hands open the cheeks of my ass, baring myself to his gaze.

I'm about to ask what he's doing when his tongue snakes over me, taunting my tight hole. My face heats with embarrassment as he continues to lick me there—where I've never even had my own fingers.

He spits on the spot between the cheeks, his fingers delving into me, opening me up for his cock. I don't know how it's going to fit. I have no idea how much it will hurt. As his two digits scissor me open, I claw at the table, trying to hold on for dear life.

His other hand snakes around to my pussy, teasing my clit as he fingers my ass. The pleasure and pain send sparks of lightning through me. Each nerve in my body is electric, shocking me with every movement he makes. My body is his toy, and he's enjoying playing with me.

"Such a pretty, dirty, little girl," he growls, spitting more saliva onto the opening. "Relax, baby girl. I'm going to make you feel so damn good." It's a promise. Yes, I'm scared, but I also want him.

He rises, his fingers gone. Then, I feel it. Cool liquid dripping onto my ass. When I cast a glance over my shoulder, I watch him pour olive oil over my body. Then the tip of his cock is there, nudging me. It requests entrance, and I breathe through the moment he pushes into me. I'm being stretched, opening to him, my body accepting.

"Fuck yes," he grinds out harshly as pain skitters up my spine. His hands massage my back and hips before finding my clit and tweaking it while pushing inch by inch into my ass.

I'm not sure I can take anymore, but I do. He keeps going. And just when my eyes roll to the back of my head, the pain and pleasure seem to merge into one intense explosion. My knees wobble as he dips his head beside mine.

"You're utterly fucking perfect," he says reverently, each word another slice to my heart. The heart that's falling so deep into his orbit. The heart that's finding love with a man who doesn't offer it back.

"Just fuck me," I retort. Love and anger, both emotions swirl through me, taunting me with what I want, but it's too far out of reach. "Just fucking make me cry."

My words are fueled with the anger gripping me. And that's when Levi finally snaps. His hips pull away, then slam back in, causing me to scream. My throat burns from the sounds he's drawing from my body.

"Do you think I don't want you?" he roars as his cock impales me. It feels like he's tearing me apart, trying to split me in half. "I fucking want you, Kristyn," he says, fucking me harder with each word. His savage is loose, forcing my hips against the edge of the table.

"Please, Levi." I don't know what I want. More. Less. Love. Hate.

"Fuck, baby girl," he growls.

"I can't."

"Yes, you fucking can," he commands. Everything is too much. Emotion. Pain and pleasure. They're all churning together in a tumultuous hurricane that's about to drag me into darkness. "Fuck." Words fall from his mouth as he finally takes me harder than I've ever felt before.

"Levi!"

"Tell me, Kristyn," he orders harshly. "Tell me what your eyes keep confessing. Say it," he grunts, slapping my ass as his fingers tug my clit and his cock tears into tight entrance. "Say it."

"I love you!" I finally cry out.

His body locks along with mine as we both find release. I come so hard, my knees give out. My body is sore, but my chest heaves with happiness and sadness all in one.

I said it.

His heated arousal fills me, spurting deep into my body. Warm arms wrap around me, pulling me impossibly closer to him. I want this, I need this. He lifts me without a word and carries me up the stairs and into the bedroom. My mouth opens to say something, but he shakes his head, his eyes boring into me.

Gently, he presses a finger to my lips, quietening any words that would've come tumbling out of my mouth. He plants a soft kiss on my cheek, then covers me with the thick comforter. It's warm in the room, but it's the gesture that makes me shiver.

He's been angry, more than I've ever seen him. The pain in his eyes is palpable. He turns, shutting the door, leaving me in his bedroom, in his bed and I wonder what the hell just happened.

My body still aches, my heart more so, it hurts because I know I can't fix him. No matter how I try, I can't change who he is, and it seems I certainly can't heal the pain inside this man. But, I can be there for him. Not only because he needs me to be, but because I find that I want to be.

My eyes close, and I allow sleep to steal me.

THIRTEEN

LEVI

THREE WEEKS.

Fifteen working days.

And each night I'm inside her, I feel more.

She told me she loved me, and I filled her with my cum. I didn't say it back. I haven't said anything about what happened that night. I haven't told her why I was so angry. It wasn't at her; it was at myself. At my feelings.

I shouldn't be fucking her more and more every day. But every morning I wake up, I find myself wanting to be near her again. Only, it's no longer about the sex. There's more. My chest is tight, my mind is no longer on bringing in clients. All I'm thinking about is more ways to make her scream my name.

What the fuck was I thinking when I decided to sink my

dick into my assistant?

Not a damn thing.

Because all my blood had found its way to my erection and she was the only thing I craved more than my next fucking breath. There's nothing more I can do now. I'm addicted, and if I go cold turkey, I lose the best thing that's happened to me since I lost the one woman who held my heart.

But why would Kristyn even want to spend time with me? She's beautiful, young, and has her whole life ahead of her. The meeting with Masterson Electronics went well. So well, I asked Kristyn to celebrate with me.

I don't do shit like this. I'm the asshole. Not the one who makes women's dreams come true. And each time she looks at me, I feel it. Her affection is growing. Her heart is no longer in her hands, but in mine. The problem is, I don't know what to do with it.

After Roger Masterson walked out and I glanced at the signed contract, I was elated. Eric will be happy with the ten million this client is bringing to the table. And when I looked at my little tease, she had happiness written all over her beautiful face.

Two bottles of champagne later, we decided to take the party to my suite. It was innocent—until I turned the music on. Kristyn decided to show me her *moves.* This included swaying her hips, rubbing her hands over her generous tits, and twirling her hair in a way that had me wanting to fist those chestnut locks and tug them back while I fucked her ruthlessly.

Of course, I couldn't resist. So, I did. But I also showed her who I really am: a man addicted to choking, fucking, and making her scream until her lungs give out. She didn't refuse me, which shocked me to shit. She is as feisty in bed as she is in the office. It turns me on to no end. After I finally got a taste of Kristyn, I doubt I'm going to want to stop.

She is everything I want, need, and more. My cock throbs at the memory of her calling me Sir while I plunged into her tight little hole. Her moans and whimpers are my fuel. A knock at the door drags me from the elicit images in my mind.

"What?" I bite out. As soon as the door swings open with a soft whoosh, I'm met with the woman in question. "Kristyn."

"Levi—Mr. Kingston, the meeting is about to start," she mumbles, a rosy blush darkening her fair skin, which only serves to remind me how beautifully she glowed as she unraveled beneath me. Her voice is tentative, wary even. And she should be. I'm so wound up, I'd easily take her on the boardroom table with everyone watching.

"Come in," I command. Her body trembles as she steps into my cavernous office. "I want you in the meeting today. You'll take notes. I want them typed up and emailed to me after. Eric will be there as well. I trust that won't be a problem?"

"Not at all. I'll get my iPad and meet you there." She smiles, lifting her big blue eyes to meet mine.

There's no doubt my girl is a filthy little slut when she wants to be. But when she's the shy, submissive woman, it intrigues me more.

She still hasn't told me why she needed the money. And each month, I send her an amount that will keep her out of the strip club. She's been negligent to tell me what she's using my money for and I know soon I'll have to decide what to do about it.

One moment of weakness in that strip club a little over two weeks ago and I'm like a horny teenager every time this woman is near me. Rising from my chair, I round my desk and shrug on my jacket, then head out the door to find her perched on her desk.

I fasten the buttons while watching her gaze rake its way over my frame. Her tongue flicks out, wetting her lips. Pink, glossy, plump. Perfect dick sucking lips.

"Are you ready?" I question as I reach her.

She nods with a smile, "Almost."

"Good, meet me there." I leave her to gather what

she needs.

As soon as I stalk into the boardroom, I find Brent sitting at the long table ringing his hands. “God, Levi, I’m fucked. I have a shipment that was meant to arrive two days ago and it’s still not here,” he hisses. He’s always fucked.

“What is it this time, Brent? You get caught fucking your mistress and didn’t sign off on time?” I chuckle, only to have him roll his eyes.

“No, Gigi told me she’s pregnant. She won’t take a paternity test. I need a court order, but I want your help. This needs to be kept quiet. My wife can’t find out. So, it’s been a tough time, and yes, I forgot to sign off.”

The man enjoys offering me more information than I need to know. I want to sigh so he knows what a disappointment he is as a man. This guy is an asshole. What I’d like to do is punch him in the dick, then tell him to stop fucking around on a beautiful woman who loves him. But if I did that, I’d lose another massive client for the company, so I sit quietly.

Eric isn't here yet, which I find strange. Perhaps he's out fucking some Barbie jail bait or taking her to school. The man is worse than I am with pussy.

I turn my attention to this asshole who's becoming tiresome. This is the fourth time in three months he's been in my office needing an urgent shipment brought in. This time, however, I'm charging him triple what we normally would. I'm tired of his bullshit.

Before I have time to respond, Kristyn walks in, sending heat surging through me. Her white blouse is almost see through and I can just make out the outline of the beautiful bra encasing her full breasts. She settles beside me, her iPad sitting on the table in front of her.

Meeting Brent's worried gaze, I lean my elbows on the table. "Let's get this show on the road. When, where, how, and what are we bringing in? Kristyn will take notes and get on booking the trucks you need."

Brent's gaze is overly appreciative of her, which

pisses me off. He's an asshole, and Kristyn doesn't need him ogling her body. She needs someone who can appreciate her. Someone who can take care of her. Like me. The thought startles the shit out of me. Brent starts his story, and my mind drifts to the night with the beauty beside me.

Kristyn's been dancing around my room for more than ten minutes. Rising from the sofa, I stalk toward her. "Do you like teasing me, Kristyn?" I growl, low and feral.

"I think you're the tease, Levi," she murmurs, desire dripping off every word. Reaching for her hips, I tug her against me. Her ass is against my crotch, the ridge of my erection nestling between those pert cheeks I've been salivating over for months.

"You sure about this? You've been teasing me all night," I growl. She shudders, turning her head so her gaze falls on mine.

"Just fuck me already, Levi," she commands, and I chuckle.

This woman is too fucking beautiful. Too perfect for me. I'll never be worthy of someone like Kristyn Marshall.

"I want you to drop your skirt and panties. Step out of them, bend over at the waist, and put your face on the bed. Reach back, open those pretty holes for me. Show me what I can take." I expect her to tell me to fuck off. This is the beginning of debasement, and as much as I love it, not many women allow me to do this—to degrade them to mere fuck toys.

However, this pretty woman obeys me with a smile. She pushes her skirt along with her panties down those long, lithe legs and steps out of them. Still wearing her black heels, she bends over, her torso on the bed, her hips at the edge.

With one beautiful, erotic movement, she spreads her legs wide, then reaches back and opens herself to me. The sight has my cock just about ready to explode. Fuck me.

"Is this what you wanted, Levi?" She moans my name like an elicit fucking promise. Oh darling, fuck yes, this is what I want.

I don't respond. Instead, I shove my shirt and boxers off

and drop them on the floor. My teeth rip the foil packet open, and I'm sheathed in seconds. Gripping her perfect hip with one hand, I fist my dick, slapping the tip on her puffy cunt. She's fucking drenched.

"Ready, Kismet?"

"Yes!" She shrieks as I thrust into her, fully seating myself. Her body tightens, sucking me into her heated core, and I don't relent. I don't do slow, sweet, love making. I fuck her. I drive her into the bed. Pin her down until she's gasping for air. I pull out and plunge back in. Deeper. Faster. Harder. A sheen of sweat on her tanned skin shimmers under the low lights. "Come. Fucking soak my dick, Kismet," I order, raising a hand and raining it down onto her ample ass.

Again, and again.

The cherry red handprint on her creamy smooth skin has my balls tightening. Marking a woman is a base need. One I crave. My hips slam into her. "Fuck!" I growl as I empty myself into the condom.

FOURTEEN

KRISTYN

"Levi?" He shakes his head and glances at me. Those brown eyes are almost black as he shifts in his seat, and I can't stop the frown on my face. "Are you okay?" He nods.

"Brent, I'll have a look at the notes and we'll set up a court date. I'll get you the court order on one condition. The next time you walk in here, and I know there'll be next time, it won't have anything to do with you fucking around on your wife."

Levi's no-nonsense tone is pure anger. He's vibrating with rage. "Yeah. Thanks, man. I've learned my lesson." The man rises and stalks toward my boss. "Thank you." They shake hands, and Brent casts me another hungry glance before leaving.

"Asshole."

"I thought he was a friend of yours?" I question. Levi pins me with a glare so fierce, I feel it right down to my core.

"I may be an asshole, Kristyn, but I've learned from my mistakes. That dick has been in here every second month with a problem, and they're normally names like Gigi, Lola, or any other exotic dancers he can find wherever he goes when his wife is alone at home."

"So, you're saying you've never slept with multiple women?" I ask on a smile. Shrugging off his jacket, he hangs it on the back of the chair, then stalks toward the door. Clicking the lock, he turns back to me.

"Get on your knees," he commands. It's an order. There's nothing about this situation that's okay. I'm his employee. He's my boss. And I have a feeling he's about to ask me to suck his cock. "Do you want me to ask you again?" he bites out angrily.

"Why are you doing this, Levi? Honestly, I can't do it

anymore. I'm not here just to take your frustrations out on. You want me on my knees to suck your dick? Then give me a reason to." My words are laced with anger. I'm about to continue, but he strides toward me. His hand is on my arm, tugging me out of the chair to stand before him. The heels I'm wearing make us almost eye to eye—the same pair I wore the first time he fucked me.

"This... I don't know what it is, but I want you. I can't stop thinking about how beautifully tight your cunt is. I can't forget how your body trembles when I make you come. And now, I'm going to do something I probably shouldn't, but I don't give a fuck anymore." With that, he spins me around and swipes his hand over the table, sending mugs and coffee flying. They land with a loud crash.

Taking the lead, he pushes my black pencil skirt up and over my hips. A vibration rumbles in his chest, low and deep. He's an animal when it comes to fucking. The scrap of material that was my panties is ripped from my body.

Then, I feel it. His hot breath. His beard. His hands.

He grips the cheeks of my ass and opens me to his gaze. It's filthy, so fucking dirty, but I'm soaked. "You're glistening. You love being filthy, don't you, Kismet?"

I can't answer, because the next second, his tongue is flattened against my core, making a long, torturous lick from my clit to my ass. I tense when he teases his tongue on the forbidden entrance. "What—?"

He growls against my sensitive flesh. A harsh spank on the cheek of my ass has me yelping. "Thankfully, this room is soundproof," he mumbles as he devours me. And I knew that, which is why I wasn't worried about being loud. Because of the legal meetings we have, it's impossible to even eavesdrop.

His tongue darts around my entrance.

Teasing. Taunting. Tasting.

My hands claw at something, anything, but I can't find purchase on the slippery mahogany. His face is buried between my legs. The ticklish sensation of his beard propels me into orbit, but it's his filthy words that send me over the edge.

"Drench me with your cum, dirty Kismet. Come for me. I want to drink every fucking drop of your sweetness." I convulse. Shockwaves shoot through me, alighting my nerves with pure lust, adrenalin...something. Stars dot the back of my eyelids as I scream his name, begging, pleading for him to stop, continue, I'm not sure what.

Moments later, when I finally come down from my high, I find Levi standing back, watching me with an elicit smirk on his lips.

"You're delicious, Kristyn. Tonight, I'm going to fuck you in every hole, and then I want to hear you tell me those three words you've been hiding since you mumbled them two weeks ago. Do you hear me?"

"Yes, Levi," is all I can offer. I'm worn out from just that few moments of bliss. He hasn't brought up the *I love you* that I'd allowed to fall from my lips. I thought he'd forgotten, or didn't hear me. But that's evidence enough that he did. I don't know if I can say it again. I'm not sure I can tell him I love him when he can't even say he likes me.

Once this month is over, I'll leave.

My father's medical bills are paid for the time being, but soon, I'll need to go back to Poison. I can't be with Levi and not give him my heart. So, I'll walk out and have strangers look at me and throw money at me instead. At least I know I can't love them.

I rise slowly, my legs still wobbly. He pulls out a pretty white pair of panties and smirks at me. "Figured you'd be needing these since I can't keep my hands off you," he hands me the underwear. Without another word, he leaves me gaping at his back. My boss just ate me until I came all over his face, then promised me another orgasm—another fuck. I pull the panties up my legs and smooth my skirt back down, hoping nobody notices the wrinkles in the material. The thong he ripped from my body is gone, and I'm certain it's merely shredded material now.

He must have it in his pocket.

Asshole.

But the problem is, I can't deny it. I want him.

The door behind me flies open and Pearson locks onto my gaze. He's flying through the office like a hurricane today, and I wonder if it has anything to do with work or there's a woman in his life.

Something tells me it's the latter. No matter how many contracts or deliveries have gone awry, he's never looked like that. Almost disheveled. I say almost because this is Eric—he's the epitome of a clean-cut asshole. His business comes first. His kids probably don't even know they have a father.

When Trevor walks into the main area of the office, the air changes. He's been one of those sweet, yet elusive men who doesn't really pay me any mind. He's handsome, distinguished almost, and I wonder what his story is. The only thing I do know is he has a lot of meetings offsite like Levi.

"Kristyn, meet me in Levi's office now," Eric grunts as he stalks by me. Frowning, I grab my notebook and pen in case he needs me to take notes. As soon as I enter the room, there's high tension racing through the air.

"This asshole is pissing me off, Kingston." Eric's eyes blaze like a blue flame in a breeze.

"I know, but there's nothing I can do about it now. Let's just finish his delivery and I'll cancel the next one. He's generally good with payment, but I'll follow up. Calm your shit, Pearson." Levi settles back against his black leather chair, watching his partner.

"Jesus." Eric rakes his fingers through his dark hair. His heated gaze falls on me, roving over every inch of my body. "I want you to set up a meeting with Masterson. Get him in this office tomorrow morning. Ensure it's in my calendar and Levi's."

I nod in response, making a note to email out the meeting request as soon as I'm back at my desk.

"Come here, baby girl," Levi calls, crooking his finger. I don't need to answer, because my feet have a mind of their own. As soon as he needs me, I'm there. "Sit here." He gestures to his lap, and I awkwardly settle with my ass on his crotch, feeling it throb below me.

"Kingston." The name is a warning on Eric's lips, but he makes no move to leave. His eyes are glued to the scene before him. I shouldn't have shut the door. Levi has worked it to his advantage.

"Why don't you calm down, Pearson?" Levi's deep rumble skates over my neck, causing me to shudder. His hands work their way to my blouse, unbuttoning it. "I know my little Kismet here likes to be seen," he says, and it's true. I came so hard the day Eric watched me bent over the desk.

"Then why don't you show me how pretty her tits are?" Eric murmurs, a sly smirk on his lips. His large hand palms the bulge clear in his gray slacks. Levi wastes no time in opening me to his best friend's gaze.

His palms cup my breasts, lifting them, squeezing them, teasing my nipples until they're hard peaks. My clit tingles and my body pulses, needing and wanting to be filled. But this isn't for me. This is for Eric and Levi.

I love being Levi's. My body is his to toy with as he needs. And the only reason I allow him to do this is because my heart is his as well.

I've said those three damning words. I've told him everything he wants to hear, but he still doesn't know about my dad. One day maybe.

"Look at Eric, baby girl. Do you want him to stroke his cock for you?" Levi questions in a low, gravelly tone. His chest vibrating against my back. "Tell me," he taunts, goading me to answer.

"Yes, I do."

I watch in awe as the man pulls his thick cock from those fancy gray slacks and fists it. His eyes are on mine, his lips curling in a smirk. Everything about him screams sex. He's sinful and filthy, and my pussy is wet.

Levi spreads my legs with his, lifting my skirt to flash my panties at Eric.

"See, Pearson, she wears these little white cotton things," Levi teases his best friend. His hand rains down a swat on my mound, harder and faster, again and again. My head drops back as pleasure takes over me. I'm drenched. He continues to spank my pussy.

"Fuck, she's beautiful." The rough, husky grunt comes from the man who's now standing closer, watching in awe as I mewl.

"Her tight little hole is soaked. Isn't it, baby girl?" Once again, his words turn me on. They send me spiraling into an abyss of need and want. I want to close my legs, I want pressure on my clit. "Suck Eric's cock. I want to see how needy you are." It's not a request.

His tone is low, domineering. I open my eyes to find the tip of Mr. Pearson's dick in my face, glistening with pre-cum. I open my mouth as he slides inside, slow and calculated. That's when Levi's fingers dip under the waistband of my panties, delving into my now soaked entrance. He pumps into me, two fingers, then three. I'm losing track of what's happening when my mind shuts down in unsurmountable pleasure as my mouth is used.

Eric grips my hair, pulling me onto his shaft. He slides into my throat, and I gag. The soft choking sounds spur Levi to add a fourth finger.

"Listen to that wet, squelching little pussy." His words filter through my mind as I continue to devour Mr. Pearson's cock. The taste of him, salty, musky, and sweet, drips onto my tongue.

His hands fist my hair, causing my scalp to sting. My eyes water as saliva drips from my chin. Suddenly, Levi's hand is sliding into me. I am so wet, it doesn't even register until he utters in my ear. "I love your stretched little cunt. It's so wet and slick for me."

I don't know what to do. Both men continue to take

me. To show me pleasure. My core tightens, pulses. I'm close.

"Come for us." I think it's Levi who speaks. My body trembles and shudders. Jet after jet of hot release shoots onto my tongue as my pussy drenches Levi's hand, lap, and the floor under his chair. My body is no longer my own. I'm limp and weightless. Pleasure is the only thing I know as I shiver from the high of my orgasm.

"Beautiful girl," Eric says, planting a kiss on my lips.

"And that's the last time you'll ever come near her," Levi warns, and I know I'm no longer just the girl he paid for sex. I'm something else entirely, if only he'd admit it.

FIFTEEN

LEVI

"COME HERE," I MURMUR.

The candles flicker around the small room, bathing us in soft yellow light. Since the scene at the office, I've been calm, relaxed, and tentative to her. I shouldn't have done what I did, but it helped me. It confirmed what I've been feeling.

I love her.

And tonight, I'll tell her.

We just finished dinner in the living room. Smoked salmon with potatoes and spinach.

Now, I've settled on the window sill in the master bedroom watching her approach me. She's dressed in a soft white sweatshirt. It hangs to her upper thighs, just long enough to tease, but short enough to offer me a view of her beautiful legs.

"You're different," she says, straddling my thighs.

I lift the wine glass, offering it to her. She takes a small sip, the Merlot glistening on her full lips. "I feel renewed," I tell her earnestly, because it's true. She's been everything to me over this past few weeks, and I don't want to let her go.

Hell, to be honest, I could propose to her right now.

But that's not what we need. Time together, just us. No fucking. No filthy words. All I want is us to be real.

"There's something I wanted to talk to you about," I murmur, planting a chaste kiss on her lips. It's the most I've given her since we started this mind fuck of a relationship.

"Don't sound so serious, Levi." She looks genuinely worried. I know she loves me, she's told me so, and I'm certain she's worried I'm leaving her. If only she knew how impossible that is.

"I've been a bastard," I start slowly.

"Yes, you have." She giggles when I glare at her. "Okay, okay. Serious face." She frowns, making her brows scrunch together in the cutest, most playful way I've seen her.

"It's been difficult for me since Abi died. I've pushed everyone away, including Ethan. My son hasn't had a father. And you deserve a man far better than me."

"I—"

I press a finger to her mouth to silence her. "Listen." It's an order, to which she nods. "That night on the kitchen table..." I start, unsure of what I want to say. Everything I want to do for her has to be perfect, even an explanation of why I was so angry.

It hurt. Everything about that night made me realize that as long as I was holding onto the idea of Abi, no one would be right. And then Kristyn stumbles into my life and I'm in her orbit twenty-four seven, needing her.

"It was the anniversary of Abi's death. I wasn't angry with you. I...I was raging at myself because it was the night I realized I'd let go of her and fallen for you."

"You didn't want to love me." It's not a question, and she's not angry. She's contemplative, and I know why. When you love someone, there's always a fear that they'll leave. Just walk out and never come back. But when that person is still around and they don't reciprocate the love, that's what hurts even more.

My father once told me the worst thing in the world is to love someone, sleep beside them, and feel more alone than if you didn't have them there.

"I didn't want to, but I didn't have a choice. Listen to me, baby girl. There's nothing in this world that's going to tear us apart. I may not propose tonight, but I want you to know I love you. With everything I have. Yes, Abi is still the woman I loved first, but she wasn't meant to fill my whole story. She was merely a chapter."

"You're so romantic when you want to be." She leans in, scrunching her nose when she presses it against mine. The woman is sexual, beautiful, and playful. And there's nothing I want more than to be with her 'til I breathe my last breath.

"Are you sure you want to meet my father?" she asks earnestly. I think she's more worried than I am.

"Of course. Although, I'm so hungry for your sweet, supple flesh, I could most probably devour you right now, then fuck you so hard you can't walk straight," I growl in her ear, reveling in the sweet tremble that races over her body. This woman is everything I've been missing and more. Offering her that money was my way of claiming her, but deep down, I knew all I had to do was ask.

"Levi, can you just allow me to get dressed," she throws back, glaring at me. Her feisty nature makes me chuckle. I love how she can be a tame kitten for me at times, and ready to tear my dick off at others.

I leave her to get ready while I settle on the sofa, swiping through my phone to find Ethan's message. He's coming home soon, and I miss him. Having Kristyn here will be strange at first, but something tells me my boy will be just fine.

He'll spend more time with Pearson's kids when he's back anyway. The five boys have been close for years. Their friendship grew from being the strangers next door to a daily visit. Since they all attend school together, they've grown even closer.

I know Ethan and Brock have been partying together, but I don't know much about the boys. It's another reason I want Ethan to study close to home so I can make up for lost time with my son. I know nothing can make up for the extent I missed, but I'll try.

"I'm ready," my baby girl announces, and I can't help eye fucking her in those skin-tight jeans. "Stop doing that. Dad's waiting for us," she admonishes me like a child, but I want it.

We take a slow drive to her childhood home, her wringing her hands in her lap.

"Are you nervous?" I ask without looking at her.

"A little. I've never brought anyone home and now when I do, it's a man who's twice my age," she says hesitantly. I don't care about any of the social taboos between us. Yes, she's young, but she's mine.

Love has no age. It's timeless, limitless. And if we're both consenting adults, I see no fucking problem.

"Stay calm. He'll love me." I wink cockily as I pull up to the drive.

When we make our way inside, I hold her hand. The whole house is bathed in a silence I've never experienced.

"It's him. Isn't it?" I glance at her, but I don't need her to respond. I already know. "The reason for the money?"

"Yes," she utters. Her body shakes, I pull her into my arms, cocooning her from the hurt, but I know I can't ease her pain like this.

"Call the hospital. Tell them he'll need a full-time nurse to get his treatments done at home," I order.

"Krys." A deep voice comes from the doorway, and

I'm met with blue eyes that match my woman's. I've been such an asshole, not caring about her personal life. But I'm here now, and there's nothing that will stop me making this right.

"Mr. Marshall, I am Levi Kingston." I offer him a hand, but the man glares at me angrily. "I'm helping Kristyn with the hospital treatments," I tell him, but he sees through my bullshit.

"Dad—"

"And I love your daughter," I spit out the words before she can say anything. "I'm perhaps not the man you saw her with, but I love her more than my next breath. And I'm here to ask your permission to one day, when the time is right, ask for her hand."

Silence hangs around us like a fucking lead weight. It feels as if my body is in free fall as this man judges me. He regards me with a critical eye, and I don't blame him. I need it. I welcome it.

"And what makes you think my girl here loves you?"

He chuckles, and Kristyn giggles. And when he smiles, he looks just like her, both with happiness crinkling the corners of their eyes.

"I do love him, Dad. I should've come to you about our relationship earlier, but—"

"Krys, let me tell you something. When you love someone, there is no right time or wrong time to do something. But when it's right, you feel it. Not in your mind, but deep down in your heart and soul. If this man..." he looks at me once more, narrowing his gaze, "if he's the one you want, then you know I love you enough to support anything you need."

"Thank you, Dad." She wraps her arms around him, giving him a hug she's probably held onto for so long. There's sadness in this place, and a man that's ill shouldn't be living in such dankness. As soon as we leave here, I'm calling my agent. She'll find Mr. Marshall an apartment close to my house.

"There's something else I needed to ask you, Mr.

Marshall." I implore him with my gaze, wanting him to understand I can't live without his daughter.

"Yes," he says, confusing me.

"What?"

"She can live with you. I'm tired of seeing my little girl sad. She deserves a life outside of this," he says, waving his hand around at the darkened living room.

"Dad, I don't—"

He pins her with a glare that shuts her up immediately. *I need to learn that,* I think, but then again, I do love spanking her little ass.

"There's no discussion, Krys. You're going to pack and I'll find something. Don't you worry about me. You've given up your life to look after your sick father, but no more. There's a man who loves you, and I want that for you."

Her big blue eyes glisten, shimmering like jewels, but she doesn't need me to comfort her right now, she needs her father. And he pulls her into a hug so fierce, she disappears in his arms.

"Thank you, Dad," she mumbles into his sweater.

His eyes meet mine, and I hold my breath. When he mouths, "*Look after her*," I nod in return. I'll do anything for her. She's mine now, and I'm never letting her go.

SIXTEEN

KRISTYN

A WARM RAY OF SUNLIGHT STREAMS THROUGH THE window as I open my eyes. It's been a month since Levi paid me to stop working at Poison. And it's taken a month for us to live together—to find happiness where we both had so much sadness in our lives.

Levi's arm is draped over my waist, his body warming me more than the sun. I'm cherished. Smiling, I roll over, finding those beautiful dark eyes staring back at me.

"That's not super creepy," I tell him, running my palm over the stubble on his jaw. His fingers dig in, tickling my middle, causing me to giggle loudly as I kick and squeal for him to quit it. He knows I'm prone to laughing fits, and he loves it.

"Ethan's back today," he tells me then.

All laughing ceases as I glare at him. "Why didn't you tell me sooner?" He shrugs. His son is coming home today, and he shrugs as if he just told me the weather.

"He's an adult. If I feel it's time for me to move on, then I move on."

"Levi, you can't expect him just to accept that there's another woman in the house," I utter, pushing off the bed before he can drag me back in. Racing for the bathroom, I slam into a solid mass of man-boy. "Shit." My hand flies to my mouth when I realize I'm standing in the hallway complete naked in front of my boyfriend's teenage son.

"Dang, my dad knows how to pick them," he teases as I fly past him in horror, my face burning red with embarrassment. When I reach the bathroom, I slam the door a little too loudly, but I don't care. All my clothes are in Levi's bedroom. What made me think I could slink around naked when he just told me Ethan is coming back?

There's a knock on the door, then Levi's voice. "Baby

girl, he's headed out to meet with friends." I jerk the door open, meeting the dark eyes of the man who's stolen my heart.

"You couldn't have warned me earlier?" I bite out, causing him to chuckle as if it's the funniest thing to happen. "This isn't a joke, Levi. He's your son. I feel..."

His hands grip my shoulders, pulling me closer. He drops his head so we're eye to eye. "He's my son. You're my woman. There's no getting around it. Either you calm down and just take each moment as it comes, or I'll have to move him into a penthouse apartment in the city where he can enjoy his college life after he gets back from his gap year in Italy." He's serious. There's nothing this man does or says that hasn't been thought out, planned, and well calculated.

"You knew he'd be back, you knew I would panic, and you made a plan, didn't you?" He nods, and the confident smirk on his face is all I need to wrap my arms around his neck and pull myself up against him.

He spins me around, his hands gripping my ass as he nestles his nose into my hair. There's something about him doing it that sets my mind at ease. It calms me. As if I'm his air and he needs me to survive.

"Now, get your pert little ass back in bed. I need some loving before Ethan gets back. Then we're having a family dinner. My son hasn't been here to see me fall in love again and I think it's time he gets to know you," he tells me, admiration in his tone. It causes my heart to sputter in my chest. "Preferably with some clothes on. I'm the only man allowed to see you naked."

"Stop being an asshole."

"It's why you love me, baby girl. After lunch, we're going to visit your dad," he informs me. I don't have a choice. This man has paid for my father to have a full-time nurse, all his treatments are covered, and he now has a comfortable apartment overlooking the ocean.

"How did I get so lucky?" I ask as he lays me down on the steel gray sheets.

He settles himself between my splayed thighs before answering. "It was Kismet."

"So, you and my dad?" Ethan turns to glance at me with those hazel eyes. He's handsome. Closer to my age than Levi is, but it no longer fazes me. I always wondered how girls choose older men, and since being with Levi, I know exactly why. I'm hooked, and I don't want to be released.

"Yeah, is that weird for you?" I ask, and he smirks. A heartbreaker in the making. Just like his father.

"Not at all. Just wondering how my dad landed such a hot chick," he says, and I can't help blushing. Definitely a heartbreaker. "He's normally sitting at home in his old man pj's, and here you are all sexy and pouty for him."

"I don't think that's a—"

"Don't worry, sweetheart, you're not my type. I prefer blondes," he tells me boldly. For an eighteen-year-old, he's cocky as shit, but with a father like Levi, I see where he gets it from. Personality from his dad, but his looks are a mix of his parents. His angular jaw, disheveled mocha hair, and that tanned skin is a perfect blend of Levi and his late wife, which makes for a good looking young man.

"I didn't mean that. You should give him more of a chance." He regards me for a moment, and I'm almost certain he's about to tell me I'm not his mother to offer advice, but he doesn't.

"Why? He's never given me a chance. All the times I told him what I wanted to do with my life, he's just ignored those and told me what *he* wants me to do."

"Parents can be difficult, there's no doubt about it, but he's only looking out for you, Ethan. He's a stubborn man, and something tells me you're more alike than you think. Why not just pull him aside and force him to listen?"

He shrugs, looking out over the view of the ocean

in the distance. He lifts the smoke to his mouth, pulling hard, making the cherry burn bright in the dimly lit sky. The clouds in the distance look almost purple as the sun sets.

"I tried, you know," he tells me. "For years, I begged him to hear me out. But I guess my immaturity shined through. I want to Trevel, I want to paint. He just doesn't get it. He's a numbers man. He enjoys the money and privilege and all I want to do is surf and paint pretty girls."

His words are filled with emotion. As if the thought of doing all that sets his heart alight. I can't help smiling. I've never had a passion for something as much as I did for my writing. But with Dad being sick, I put all that on hold. Yes, I have studied, but it wasn't to do what my heart desires. For too long, I listened to everyone else.

Hearing Ethan speak so passionately about what he wants only seems to light a fire inside me.

"I can talk to him," I offer. Leaning over, I try to get him to look at me, but he doesn't. He watches the waves.

"Is there a girl in the picture?"

"No. She left." He doesn't sound too sad about it and I wonder if it was just a fling or something more. "There are times I wonder what would've happened if she had stayed. But I know sometimes moving on is the best for both people," he says, sounding far older than he is.

"Did your dad tell you that?" He nods. "I guess it's true. But sometimes the heart wants that first person." He turns to me, his mouth curving into a lopsided grin. "And anyway, you're far too handsome to be locked down to one girl. There are so many out there, you'll find her."

"Are you flirting with me, Kristy?" he chuckles, as he calls me by the nickname he's gifted me.

"No, don't be an ass," I retort, swatting him on the bare shoulder. He came back an hour ago from surfing and he's dressed only in board shorts. "I just mean, there are other girls out there who may come into your life and you'll fall in love again."

"Oh, no. There's no way I'm falling in love. Right

now, all I want is a nice tight pussy to fuck." His vulgar response has me gasping. But I shouldn't be too shocked. He's definitely his father's son.

"If you keep talking like that, you'll never find a girl." I admonish, but he laughs as if I'm the funniest person on earth.

"Listen to the hypocrite," he says in shock. "I've heard you and my dad going at it like bunnies." He causes me to choke on my retort.

"That's creepy, you know," I tell him. "Listening to us."

"Can't help it. I'm a young, virile man." He winks, rising from the chair. "And let me tell you something, listening to the two of you is better than any porno. Who knew my dad had that much energy?"

He leaves me gaping at his retreating form as he races down the wooden steps and onto the private beach behind Levi's home.

"You're an asshole!" I call out, earning me a satisfied

wave. He disappears from sight and I'm left alone for a moment. Levi will be home any minute and I need to get ready. There's a meeting he wants me to attend with him and I recall the last time we had one.

He took me to the beach and we made love violently. It was passionate and raw. He broke me open so many times, but each time, he put me back together. He's been my glue at the toughest moments over the past month.

There's just so much more to Levi Kingston than all the money he has, or the home and cars. He plays the cold-hearted bastard in the boardroom, and in the beginning, he did it in the bedroom too. Even in his most closed off moments, I found him lurking beneath the façade.

All the material items are nothing compared to the heart beating in his chest. He may hide it away most times, but I know the real him.

And that's the man I love.

ENJOYED THIS BOOK?

MEET THE OTHER FATHERS

Four Fathers Series by bestselling authors

J.D. Hollyfield, Dani René,

K Webster, and Ker Dukey

Four genres.

Four bestselling authors.

Four different stories.

Four weeks in April.

One intense, sexy,

thrilling ride from beginning to end!

****These books were designed so you can read them out of order. However, they each interconnect and would be best enjoyed by reading them all!****

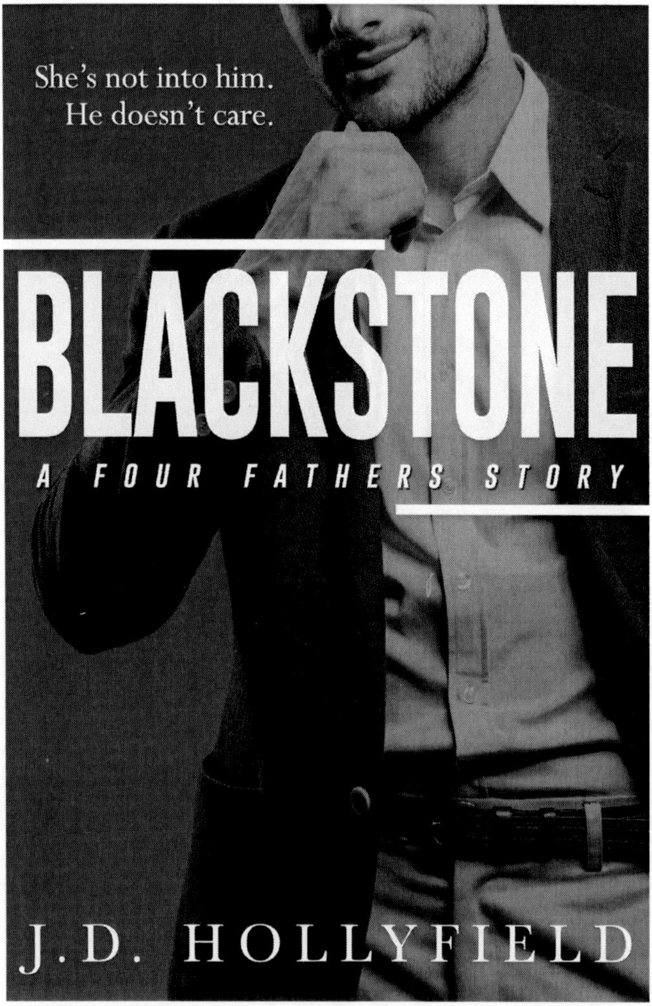
She's not into him.
He doesn't care.
BLACKSTONE
A FOUR FATHERS STORY
J.D. HOLLYFIELD

OTHER BOOKS IN THE
FOUR FATHERS SERIES

BLACKSTONE
BY J.D. HOLLYFIELD

Contemporary Romance

I am meticulous. Structured. A single father.
I obsess over things and crave control.
And when a hot, feisty little woman throws a wrench in my carefully laid out plans, I lose my mind.
My every thought revolves around making her bend to my will—until they become less about her doing things my way and more about just her.
My name is Trevor Blackstone.
I am an obsessive, complicated, demanding man.
People may not understand me, but it doesn't stop them from wanting me.

PEARSON
A FOUR FATHERS STORY
She's too young for him.
He doesn't care.
K WEBSTER

OTHER BOOKS IN THE
FOUR FATHERS SERIES

PEARSON
BY K WEBSTER

Taboo Romance

I am selfish. Spoiled. A single father.
I do what I want because I can.
One of my four sons is dating the hot,
young little neighbor...
Too bad it won't last long.
When I want something, I take it—even if it means
taking from my son.
My name is Eric Pearson.
I am an unapologetic, egotistical, domineering man.
People may not like me, but it doesn't stop them from
wanting me.

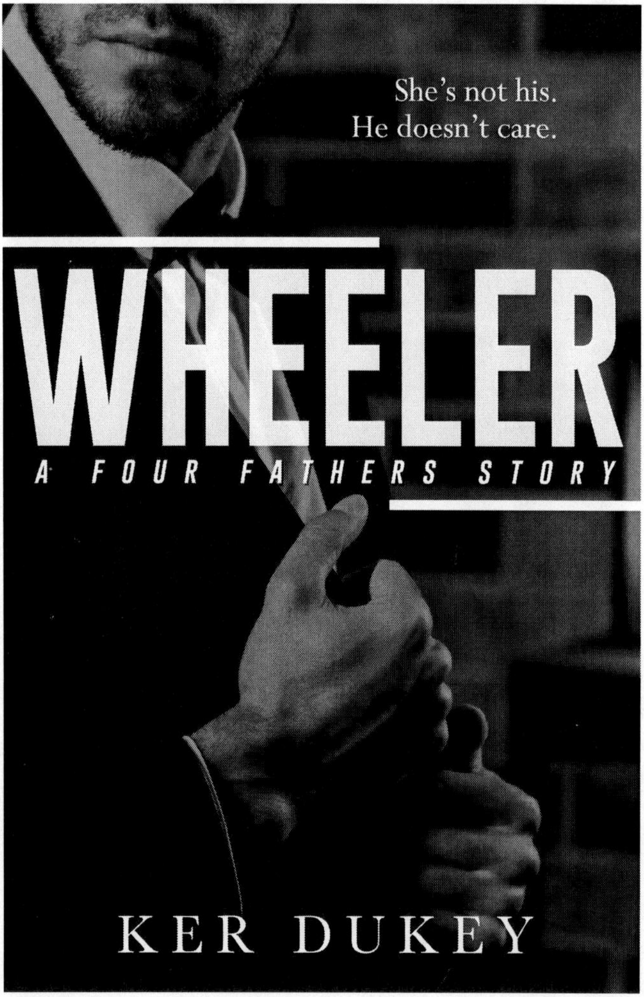
She's not his.
He doesn't care.
WHEELER
A FOUR FATHERS STORY
KER DUKEY

OTHER BOOKS IN THE

FOUR FATHERS SERIES

WHEELER

BY KER DUKEY

Dark Suspense

I am dark. Calculating. A single father.
I have secrets that would horrify most people.
Stalking is a habit I refuse to break—and what happens after is a sweet reward.
My life is exactly the way I have designed it.
But an undeserving, sick monster is dating my only daughter.
Until I deal with my problem, I can't truly enjoy everything I've created.
My name is Jax Wheeler.
I'm a twisted, evil, insane man.
People may be afraid of me,
but it doesn't stop them from wanting me.

ACKNOWLEDGMENTS

Thank you to my amazing friend K Webster for inviting me to join this amazing project. You're an incredible inspiration and I'm so excited to be able to call on you for advice.

To Jess (J.D. Hollyfield) and Ker Dukey, it's been such fun working with you both on this project. You ladies rock!

Thank you to Monica for editing and polishing Kingston and for loving this filthy man. xx

To my Darklings reader group, thank you for the support and love you show on a daily basis. You're my rockstars!!

To my author colleagues, thank you for being there and sharing my books, and offering the support in this crazy journey.

To the bloggers, thank you a million times over for supporting me. By reading, reviewing, and sharing, you ladies make this dream of mine possible!

To my readers, thank you for always trusting me and reading my words. Hugs and love xx

ABOUT DANI

Dani is an international bestselling author and proud member of the Romance Writer's Organization of South Africa.

A fan of dark romance that grabs you by the throat and doesn't let go. It's from this passion that her writing has evolved from sweet and romantic, to dark and delicious. It's in this world she's found her calling, growing from strength to strength and hitting her stride.

On a daily basis, she has a few hundred characters, storylines, and ideas floating around in her head. From the feisty heroines she delivers to the dark, dominant alphas that grace the pages of her books, she promises light in a world filled with danger and darkness.

She has a healthy addiction to reading, TV series, music, tattoos, chocolate, and ice cream.

OTHER BOOKS

Standalones

Ace of Harts

Love Beyond Words

CUFFED

Fragile Innocence

Taboo Novellas

His Temptation

Austin's Christmas Shortcake

Crime & Punisment (Newsletter Exclusive)

Ink Duet

Pierced Ink

Madd Ink

Broken Series

Broken by Desire

Shattered by Love

Anthologies

Infamous Hearts

OTHER BOOKS

Sirens of SaSS

The Backstage Series

Between Love & Fire

Between Lust & Tears

Between Want & Fear

Backstage Boxset (Books 1-3)

Forbidden Series

From the Ashes - A Prequel

Crave (Book #1)

Covet (Book #2)

Sins of Seven Series

Kneel (Book #1)

Whisper (Book #2)

Indulge (Book #3)

Coloring Books

Shaded by Love Volume 5

Made in United States
North Haven, CT
04 April 2023

34965533R00111